The alien posse closed in...

Rico was a big man, a friend who had fought at McCade's side many times and who rarely ran from anything. But as he spun his animal around, Rico saw the situation was hopeless. The posse was closer now, only a thousand yards away, and if it came to a fight, the two of them wouldn't stand a chance.

Rico tossed McCade an informal salute and shouted, "Keep an eye peeled, ol' sport, I'll be back." Then he wheeled his bouncer and took off.

The mob was closer now with only the narrowness of the street to slow them down. It was a thundering mass that rippled up and down as it moved.

McCade drew his weapon and fired over their heads. Suddenly the mob came apart. But they were back moments later, brandishing a wild variety of hardware and screaming at the top of their lungs.

McCade was lying facedown spread-eagled on the pavement. He hoped they'd take him alive.

ALIEN BOUNTY

WILLIAM C. DIETZ

ACE BOOKS, NEW YORK

This one is for the guys:
Ron Crawford, Steve Bachelder,
Mike Davison, Rion Dudley,
Ron Hand, Nick Kirchoff,
Jim Potter, George Rigg, Craig Riss,
Marvin Straus, and Joe Walsh.

ALIEN BOUNTY

One

"PRISONER MCCADE!" THE guard's voice cut through the soft murmur like a knife. What light there was glazed the surface of things and left the rest dark.

The other prisoners drifted away leaving McCade to stand alone. They had enough trouble without borrowing any of his.

McCade was dirty, his leathers were ripped, and his black hair fell down around his shoulders in thick, greasy coils. But there was no fear in his cool gray eyes or in the set of his long, lean body.

The guard shifted his considerable weight from one foot to the other and gripped the nerve lash more tightly. "Are you McCade?"

McCade smiled. "No . . . I'm Grand Admiral Keaton. Is my fleet ready?"

A wide variety of rude noises issued forth from the surrounding darkness. Behind his face shield the guard flushed. "Very funny, pit slime. Now move."

McCade obeyed. Something heavy fell into his stomach as he stepped aboard the lift disk. Bad though Pit 47 was, there'd been reason to hope. Maybe Rico would come back. Maybe he'd escape slavery in the mines. But that was gone now. Each day the guards took one or two prisoners away and now it was his turn.

"Hands."

McCade held out both hands, wrists touching. The guard gave a grunt of satisfaction as he locked the nerve shackles in place. Any attempt to remove them would result in unbelievable agony.

The guard was a big man with thick eyebrows, meaty lips, and an enormous jaw. "This is Duncan in Pit 47. I've got prisoner McCade on disk two."

The voice in his ear was bored. "Code."

Duncan subvocalized so McCade couldn't hear. "Mary four Mary."

"Roger."

The disk hummed softly as it floated them upward. It, and another just like it, were the only way in or out of Pit 47. Each disk would lift two, and only two, people. Even if the prisoners killed the pit guards and took both disks, only four of them could lift. And without the proper code they'd be killed long before they reached the reception station up above.

The anti-grav disks were expensive, but what the hell, the Molarians had credits to burn. Molaria was the single known source of Nerlinium Crystals, and as everyone knows, Nerlinium Crystals are a very important component in hyperdrives.

Molaria was an artifact world, one of the mysterious planets once home to a long-vanished race, now part of the human empire. Having learned the secrets of hyperdrive from artifacts the aliens had left behind, humans had also discovered the value of the ancient mines that dotted the surface of Molaria. From those mines came Nerlinium Crystals, and from the crystals came untold wealth, some of which had gone into lift disks for Pit 47.

All of which did very little to comfort Sam McCade as the disk carried him upward. More than a hundred feet of

smooth featureless wall went by before the disk stopped and
the guard motioned for him to get off.

A muscle in his left cheek began to twitch as McCade
stepped off the disk. He'd been in a lot of tight spots during
his years as a bounty hunter, but this was one of the tightest.
What had started out as a routine trip to buy some spare
drive crystals had turned into a nightmare.

After a routine landing he and Rico had approached a
crystal dealer with a perfectly reasonable offer. She'd coun-
tered with an attempt to rob them, and even though they
managed to escape, both men were soon running for their
lives.

Running out of her store, they spotted three of the local
riding animals. Having climbed aboard two of the creatures,
they shot the third in a futile attempt to delay pursuit and
headed for the spaceport at top speed. Once aboard Mc-
Cade's ship they stood a good chance of getting off-planet
alive. *Pegasus* was well armed and damned fast.

But they'd have to get there first and that wouldn't be
easy. Like most dealers this one had her own security guards
and they gave chase. Minutes later the guards were joined
by a squad of Molarian mounted police and a posse of
bloodthirsty citizens, all of whom were experts at riding
their three-legged bouncers.

Each of the sauroids has two powerful hind legs and a
single foreleg located at the center of its chest. As the rear
legs push off the foreleg functions as a pivot bearing the
animal's weight until the hind legs hit the ground again. As
a result the animals bounce up and down, which explains
both their name and why it takes some practice to ride them.

McCade was thrown off time after time. The falls hurt
and burned precious seconds at the same time. Seconds they
desperately needed to reach the spaceport in time.

Maybe it was his childhood on a farm, or the many years
spent living on primitive worlds, but whatever the reason
Rico took to the bouncers naturally. He seemed glued to
the plastic saddle as he shouted for people to get out of the
way and led McCade through a maze of side streets.

But their pursuers were catching up and as McCade went down for the sixth time he yelled for Rico to leave him.

Rico was a big man, a friend who had fought at McCade's side many times and who rarely ran from anything. But as he spun his animal around, Rico saw the situation was hopeless. The posse was closer now, only a thousand yards away, and if it came to a fight, the two of them wouldn't stand a chance.

Rico tossed McCade an informal salute and shouted, "Keep an eye peeled, ol' sport, I'll be back." Then he wheeled his bouncer and took off.

The mob was closer now with only the narrowness of the street to slow them down. It was a thundering mass that rippled up and down as it moved.

McCade drew his weapon and fired over their heads. Suddenly the mob came apart as groups of riders spurted into side streets and alleys.

But they were back moments later brandishing a wild variety of hardware and screaming at the top of their lungs. But Rico had a good head start by this time and McCade was lying face-down spread-eagled on the pavement. He hoped they'd take him alive.

And they had, though not without a beating, and a quick trip to Pit 47. All for nothing though, since Rico hadn't come back, and they were taking him to God knows where.

"Strip."

McCade did as he was told, stripping off his leathers and submitting to a body search. There were four guards now and they were visibly disappointed when they failed to turn up a homemade blaster or nuclear warhead. Something like that would justify a beating and beatings were their main source of entertainment.

They shoved him into a cubicle with a lot more force than was necessary and slammed the door. It was small and dark like the inside of a coffin. McCade was about to attack the door when a red light came on and a hard spray hit him from every direction. The dirt seemed to slide off his skin and the spray reeked of disinfectant.

McCade gave a sigh of relief. It was some sort of de-contamination booth. They didn't want him spreading any nasty diseases to the good citizens of Molaria.

When the chemical bath was over the booth beeped and the door popped open. McCade felt very naked as he stepped outside.

"Come on, pit slime." It was the guard with the enormous jaw.

"How 'bout my clothes?"

"Clothes?" the guard asked with a big grin. "You don't need clothes. You're beautiful just the way you are. Isn't that right, guys?"

There was a loud chorus of guffaws and rude suggestions as the other guards assured McCade that he didn't need any clothes.

"Move." The word was accompanied by a shove between the shoulder blades.

McCade moved. The guard with the enormous jaw walked in front with a second guard following along behind. The second guard enjoyed prodding McCade with the handle of his nerve lash.

At first there wasn't much to see, just the perfect smoothness of ancient walls and the guard posts located by each pit.

The pits were vertical shafts that the long-lost aliens had drilled searching for crystals. Being a practical people, the citizens of Molaria had put the shafts to use. All it took was a small investment of time and energy to make them into excellent holding pens. A lighted sign marked each pit head, and McCade noticed that the numbers were getting smaller, twenty-one, twenty, nineteen, and so on.

The numbers eventually dwindled away, four, three, two, one, and a bank of lift tubes. One was designated "Prisoners Only," and that was the one they stepped into.

The platform carried them smoothly upward and stopped at a busy corridor. McCade recognized one of the main subsurface tunnels that crisscrossed Molaria Prime.

The city had three distinct levels. The surface where

McCade was captured, the subsurface level where he was now, and the deeps where he would go next.

That's where the slaves worked, lungs gasping for breath, eyes bulging as they searched for the glitter of a Nerlinium Crystal in the dark matrix of ancient rock. A crystal meant a double ration of food, a day off, and sex for those who still cared.

But all that was invisible up here where well-dressed citizens strolled the brightly lit tunnels talking business or just killing time.

McCade felt completely and terribly exposed as the guards led him out into the tunnel. He thought all eyes were on him at first, seeing his nakedness, his complete vulnerability. But then he noticed how their eyes slid past him to look at something else. They didn't *want* to see him. He might remind them of the slaves, of the crystals they scratched from the rock, and the tainted money that flowed into their hungry pockets. No, it was better not to see, not to know where the naked man was going or what would happen to him.

McCade wondered if he'd done the same thing. He too had walked these halls and for the life of him couldn't remember any naked prisoners. Had he tuned them out? Too busy with his own affairs to really see? He couldn't be sure.

McCade forced his head up, straightened his back, and put a spring into his step. He made it a point to meet their eyes and smile. Maybe one of them would see and remember.

The guards led him through a maze of tunnels and corridors until they arrived in front of a steel gate. A pair of guards lounged to either side, their blast rifles hung on slings, their visors tilted up and back. The smaller of the two spoke. "What's this, Dunc? More pit slime?"

Duncan nodded as the other guards opened the gate and shoved McCade inside. "That's about the size of it, Mac. You'll like him. He's got a sense of humor."

"Oh, goody," Mac said approvingly. "Maybe he'll tell

the judge some jokes. The judge likes jokes.''

Duncan laughed and slapped Mac on the back. "Take care, Mac . . . I'll see you at shift end.''

"Sounds good,'' Mac replied. "You can buy me a beer.''

Duncan waved as he walked away, secretly glad to be rid of the man with the gray eyes, and ashamed of feeling that way. The man scared him, and since *he* was the one with the nerve lash, that didn't seem right.

The gate crashed closed and McCade found himself in a tiled room. A stiff spray lanced down to sting his skin and wash the slime off his feet.

Sixty seconds later the water stopped, a beeper beeped, and a door hissed open. "Prisoner McCade, step forward and be judged.'' The voice came from nowhere and everywhere at once.

There was little point in doing otherwise. McCade stepped through the door and found himself in a large, noisy room.

To the left, row after row of shabby theater-style seats slanted up to a dingy ceiling. The aisles were filled with garbage, and for that matter so were the seats, for McCade had never seen a sleazier crowd.

There were spacers waiting for an outbound berth, prospectors building a new stake, and even a sprinkling of aliens doing God knows what. All were talking, gesturing, and loudly vying for one another's attention. McCade felt like the main attraction at a Roman circus.

A raised platform stood off to the right. On it there was a formal-looking desk, and behind the desk there was a vast fat man, busily eating a large meal. At the moment his greasy fingers were busily dismembering a small carcass. The scattering of bones around his chair suggested that the meal had been under way for some time.

A quick check of the audience revealed that many of them were similarly engaged, although at least one pair of Zords seemed to be making love, though it's hard to tell with Zords. To the untrained eye Zordian sex acts look very similar to the ritual wrestling patterns they use to mark the summer solstice.

McCade looked for somewhere to go, something to do, but a burly guard shook his head. So he stood there instead, shivering under a cold air vent, and hoping the fat man would choke on a bone. He didn't.

He ate until the food was gone, belched his approval, and tossed his plate aside. Then he wiped his fingers on the front of his robe, blew his nose, and cleared his throat.

This was such an obvious signal that McCade expected the crowd to quiet down. But they didn't and the noise continued unabated.

The fat man frowned. Reaching inside his robes, he brought out a huge slug gun. Pointing it toward the audience, he pulled the trigger. The gun roared and a pimp sitting in the last row lost his hat.

The room fell silent. The fat man grinned his satisfaction and made the gun disappear. "That's better. We'll have order in this court or I'll know the reason why."

The fat man picked up a print-out, blew the crumbs off it, and turned toward McCade. "My name's Benjamin Borga, a duly qualified judge in the courts of Molaria and a helluva nice guy."

Borga turned his attention back to the print-out without waiting for McCade's response. "Let the record show that one Sam McCade stands before the court accused of serious crimes and subject to Molarian law."

Here Borga paused and smiled at the crowd. They cheered in anticipation of what he'd say next. "Also present is a jury of McCade's peers, duly sworn in and ready to earn the princely sum of fifty credits for a hard day's work."

The crowd cheered even louder.

Now McCade understood. The crowd was a paid jury. That's why it was heavily loaded with indigents, drifters, and petty criminals.

"The law clerk will now read a list of McCade's crimes."

The stentorian voice was back, and this time McCade realized it was a computer, and a somewhat pompous computer at that.

"Citizen Sam McCade stands accused of attempted fraud,

animal theft, destruction of private property, reckless riding, felonious flight from the law, attempted murder, resisting arrest, and disrespect for an officer of the law.''

Borga slumped back in his chair and stared at the ceiling. "So, McCade, how do you plead?''

McCade looked around. Some of the so-called jurors were still eating, others were asleep, and the rest were talking among themselves. The whole thing was a joke. He was about to say so when the courtroom doors burst open, a section leader yelled, "Freeze!'' and twenty Imperial Marines trotted into the room.

They wore full armor and carried their blast rifles at port arms. Within seconds they had established interlocking lines of fire that covered the entire audience.

An uneasy murmur swept through the crowd. Some of the jurors got up to leave but took their seats again when the section leader used his energy rifle to punch holes in the durocrete wall over their heads.

A tall, slim man strode into the courtroom a few seconds later. He wore armor with the stars of a full admiral welded to both shoulder plates and carried a helmet tucked under his right arm. He was good-looking in a carefully groomed way, and as he approached the bench, he surveyed the room with obvious distaste.

Borga was on his feet. His face was beet red and his piggy little eyes glared with malevolence. "Who the hell are you? How dare you invade my courtroom? I demand to know the meaning of this!''

The admiral stopped, looked at Borga, and frowned. "It *means* that you are in deep trouble. My name is Swanson-Pierce. Now shut up and sit down.''

Swanson-Pierce turned toward McCade. "Hello, Sam.'' He looked the bounty hunter up and down. "You've never been an example of sartorial elegance . . . but this is absurd.''

Two

SWANSON-PIERCE GAVE McCade a VIP cabin and a robo steward called "Slider." Thus equipped he ate and slept his way through two planetary rotations. The weeks in Pit 47 had taken their toll. He was tired and unendingly hungry.

It became a routine. He'd wake up, eat the food Slider brought, and go back to sleep. But the periods of sleep became shorter and shorter as time passed until he finally rolled out of bed early in the third rotation.

He took a shower, put on a set of new leathers, and lit his first cigar in months. He took a drag and decided the cigar was a bit on the sweet side. But sweet or not the cigar was free so what the hell. McCade settled into a comfortable chair and blew a long, thin streamer of smoke toward the overhead.

Slider extruded an olfactory sensor, detected airborne impurities, and sprayed the air with deodorant. As with most military robots, form had been allowed to follow function and Slider looked like a box on wheels. "I'm sorry about the smell, sir. I'll notify the ship's atmospheric control center if it's bothering you."

McCade smiled. "Thanks, Slider, but that won't be necessary. I like the smell. That's why I set these things on fire."

"Oh," the robot replied, "I understand," although it was quite clear that he didn't.

The intercom chimed and faded up from black. Swanson-Pierce was at his impeccable best. His space-black uniform was completely unadorned except for the gold stars that marked his rank. "So you're up and around. I must say you look better with some clothes on."

"And I'm warmer too," McCade replied. "Thanks for the timely court appearance. You made one helluva character witness."

"It was my pleasure," Swanson-Pierce replied solemnly, and McCade knew he was telling the truth. The two of them went way back and the relationship was anything but friendly. Finding McCade naked in the middle of a courtroom was a dream come true, an incident Swanson-Pierce would hold over his head for years to come.

A new belt and holster hung from the arm of his chair. McCade pulled the Molg-Sader recoilless from its oiled leather and aimed at the screen. "And there's all the goodies you've been handing out. I guess I should thank you for those as well."

The naval officer lifted a single eyebrow and smiled.

As McCade lowered the gun he knew the bastard was up to something. The VIP cabin, the cigars, the new handgun, it was all part of an effort to soften him up. Make him willing to do something. The question was what.

McCade forced a smile. "How's Rico? I assume he's the one who told you where I was."

The naval officer nodded. "Rico's just fine. As usual he's down in the officer's mess eating. Just a moment. I have a surprise for you."

Swanson-Pierce stepped out and Sara stepped in. She held Molly in her arms. Both were smiling.

Sara was beautiful. A softly rounded face, large hazel eyes, and full red lips. He no longer saw the scar that slashed down across her face. Like the battle that had caused it, the scar was part of the past.

Both were satisfied to simply take each other in for a moment. Then Molly waved her chubby arms, kicked her legs, and said, "Gaaa!"

Sara laughed, McCade grinned, and Molly gurgled.

Swanson-Pierce stepped into the picture and smiled. "We sent a destroyer to get Sara, and a good thing too. She was getting ready to come after you. Why don't you join us? Your robo steward will show you the way."

McCade stared at the screen for a full minute after it had faded to black. It was wonderful to see his family again, but why all the hospitality?

Yes, he had some friends in high places, including the Emperor himself. After the second Emperor's death Princess Claudia had tried to usurp her brother's place, and would have, if McCade hadn't tracked Alexander down and helped him to assume the throne.

Knowing that, Rico had used his friend's relationship with the Emperor to summon help. Allright fine, but why the VIP treatment? And why bring his family from Alice?

Well, there was no point in putting off the inevitable, and besides, Sara was waiting. With Slider out front to lead the way, McCade took to the ship's busy corridors.

McCade's leathers were those of an officer, and even though he wore no badges of rank, he was on the receiving end of more than a few salutes. It brought back memories of a younger time when he'd worn lieutenant's bars and the wings of an interceptor pilot. Of a time when he'd blasted out to fight the pirates off the planet Hell.

They'd called themselves rebels back then, the stubborn remnants of a larger force that had been all but wiped out during a protracted civil war. Refusing the first Emperor's rule, they had forced one last battle and McCade had been there.

He could see the pirate ship locked in the electronic cross hairs of his sight, feel the firing stud under his thumb, and hear the pirate's desperate voice. "Please, in the name of whatever gods you worship, I implore you, don't fire! My ship is unarmed. I have only women, children, and old men aboard . . . Please listen to me!''

McCade could hear the second voice as well, Captain Ian Bridger's voice as he screamed: "Fire, Lieutenant! That's an order! She's lying. Fire, damn you!"

But McCade had refused. And in doing so he ended his naval career and wound up as a bounty hunter.

An interstellar police force would cost a great deal of money, so interplanetary law enforcement was carried out by bounty hunters, men and women who pursued fugitives for a price. They were a strange breed hated by those they sought and feared by those they served. The perfect profession for a cashiered naval officer in need of funds.

So when Ian Bridger uncovered the existence of an artifact planet called the "War World," and decided to give its secrets to the alien Il Ronn, Admiral Keaton had asked McCade to track him down. McCade met Bridger's daughter Sara in the process, fell in love, and settled on Alice.

Slider arrived at a busy intersection, tried to stop, and slid into a burly chief petty officer. The CPO lost his balance, his omnipresent coffee cup, and a considerable amount of his dignity as he hit the deck.

The chief scrambled to his feet, kicked Slider in the rear power port, and stalked off down the corridor.

McCade helped the robot back onto its rollers. "Don't tell me, let me guess. This is why they call you Slider."

Slider nodded his torso miserably. "I'm afraid so. It's very disconcerting. Robotech Hu can't find the problem."

"Well, it could be worse," McCade said. "At least they think you're worth fixing."

Slider was silent for a moment and then seemed to brighten up. "That *is* good, isn't it?"

McCade nodded. "It sure beats a future in the spare parts business."

From there it was a short walk to Swanson-Pierce's day cabin. A pair of marines stood guarding the door. They snapped to attention as McCade approached, and waved him inside. He was surrounded by people the moment he stepped through the hatch.

Rico was there, slapping him on the back and saying, "Good ta see ya, ol' sport."

Sara was in his arms seconds later, her eyes large with concern, the clean smell of her filling his nostrils. "Are you all right? You look so skinny."

As their lips met McCade felt two little arms wrap themselves around his right leg. Looking down, he saw two bright eyes, a mop of brown hair, and a big grin. "Da?"

McCade scooped Molly up into a three-way hug, kissed her, and laughed as she grabbed his nose.

Glancing toward Swanson-Pierce, he saw something completely unexpected. A look of envy. It reminded him that there was a man under that uniform, a man who'd never been married, and had only his career to keep him warm at night.

He shook the feeling off. When Swanson-Pierce wanted something he'd use anything to get it, including McCade's sympathy if he knew it existed.

Swanson-Pierce smiled and gestured toward some comfortable-looking furniture. "Have a seat, Sam . . . I rarely get a visit from friends . . . so this was too good to pass up."

"It's hard to visit with something you don't have," McCade mumbled under his breath.

Swanson-Pierce ignored it, Rico grinned, and Sara gave him a sharp look as they took their seats.

There was a wall-sized viewscreen behind the naval officer. Molaria was a brown ball marbled with white clouds and streaked with blue. It hung in the middle of the viewscreen like a painting in a frame.

The naval officer saw McCade's look and pointed a thumb over his right shoulder. "Things have changed since you left. A marine division went dirtside two rotations ago. They've taken control of the government, the armed forces, and the judicial system."

Swanson-Pierce smiled. "Judge Borga is looking for Nerlinium Crystals in the deeps, his so-called jury has been dismissed, and we're sorting out the people in the pits. We've known about Molaria for some time. Your situation gave us a good excuse to move in and clean things up.''

McCade felt a strange sense of pride. Since taking the throne, Alexander had launched a concerted effort to clean up some of the worst planetary governments. The effort was long overdue, and while McCade couldn't take credit for that, he'd certainly helped make it possible.

"How is Alex anyway?"

The naval officer winced. No one else would dare refer to the prince as "Alex," but it wouldn't do any good to complain, since McCade had permission from the Emperor himself.

"Just fine. As you know he and Lady Linnea are married now, and she's expecting. They both send their best."

McCade nodded. "They're good people. Maybe there's hope for us yet."

Swanson-Pierce was strangely quiet as he reached inside his jacket and brought out a sealed envelope. Wordlessly he handed the envelope to McCade.

The envelope bore the Imperial crest, Alexander's seal, and McCade's name. He opened the envelope and, with Sara looking over his shoulder, read the contents.

Dear Sam,

I was sorry to hear about your problems on Molaria, but Walter will sort it out and probably rub you the wrong way in the process. Please forgive him. He acts in my behalf, and pompous though he may be, Walter is doing a great deal to hold the Empire together. And God knows the Empire is all that stands between us and final darkness.

We need time, Sam, time to make it stronger, and time to make it better. I know you have no love for empires, ours or theirs, but consider the alternatives. Entire worlds burned down to bare rock, billions of lives lost, and a future filled with tyranny. So if Walter asks for a favor, listen, and if you won't do it for him, then please do it for me.

Regardless of what you decide, anything within my power is yours, and that includes my friendship.

Alex

A host of thoughts swirled through McCade's mind as he tucked the note into its envelope. So there *was* more to his rescue than an Imperial favor. Alexander had a problem, a problem he hoped McCade could solve, a problem that threatened the Empire.

McCade felt mixed emotions. Resentment toward another intrusion into his life, fear of what the task might entail, and yes, like it or not, a rising sense of excitement.

Swanson-Pierce tried to hide his curiosity as McCade lit the envelope and turned a cigar over the resulting flame.

When the cigar was drawing to his satisfaction, McCade dropped the remains of the envelope into an ashtray and allowed the flame to burn itself out. Molly made a dash for the ashtray and McCade picked her up. "Alex says you have a problem."

The naval officer nodded and flicked an invisible piece of lint off his sleeve. "I suppose you could call it 'a problem' though that might understate things a bit. You'll recall our policy regarding the pirates?"

Sara spoke for him. Her voice was grim. "You bet we do. We think of it every time they attack, every time they steal our supplies, and every time they kill more of our friends."

As head of Alice's planetary council Sara had strong feelings about the pirates. Although the rebel forces had been defeated in the Battle of Hell, some had escaped and taken to piracy along the rim. Alice and the rest of the rim worlds were the constant victims of their raids.

However, the pirates had one redeeming virtue, and that

was their antipathy toward the Il Ronn, something the Imperial Government used to its advantage.

Mankind had encountered many alien races among the stars but only the Il Ronn had an empire to rival their own. The Il Ronn were an ancient race, much older than mankind, and were already traveling between the stars when humans had lived in caves. Had they shared mankind's impetuous nature, they might have rolled over Terra and kept right on going.

But theirs was a slow and methodical culture based on consensus and dedicated to predictable outcomes. So while their empire grew, it did so in a slow and conservative manner.

Humans by contrast moved ahead in great spurts, leaping from caves into space in a geological twinkling of an eye, before spreading outward to settle hundreds of star systems. Unfortunately, however, huge gains were often lost through internal dissension and laziness.

The net result was two empires of roughly equal size, each eager to better itself, and to do so at the other's expense.

So both sides staged occasional raids but stopped short of all-out war. A war which neither side was sure it could win.

And that's where the pirates came in. Living as they did out along the rim, the pirates helped keep the Il Ronnians in check. That meant a smaller navy, lower taxes, and happy citizens. It also meant eternal victimization for the rim worlds.

Year after year the colonists struggled to make a living, and then, just when it seemed they'd made some headway, the pirates would come to take it all away.

It made them angry and that's why Sara's eyes burned with hatred, her hands gripped the armrest of her chair, and Molly looked up with concern. The pirate raids were something every rim worlder agreed on.

Swanson-Pierce held up a hand in protest. "I agree, believe me. If I had my way, we'd clean out the pirates and live with the higher taxes. But things aren't that simple. If

Alexander raises taxes his sister Claudia will use them to build political support for herself, and that could lead to civil war.''

"So we're damned if we do, and damned if we don't," Rico added philosophically, lighting a cigar of his own.

The naval officer shrugged. "I'm afraid so. But our present problem is even worse. The pirates staged a major raid into Il Ronnian territory not long ago. Apparently they caught the Il Ronnians napping because they managed to loot a small city and escaped with minimal losses."

Swanson-Pierce paused for a moment, looking at each of them in turn, adding weight to his next words. "And among their loot was an Il Ronnian religious relic. A relic so precious that our pointy-tailed friends are preparing a holy war to get it back."

The cabin was silent for a moment until Molly saw her mother's expression and started to cry.

Three

MCCADE AWOKE IN a cold sweat. He was surprised to be alive. The dream had been so real, so intense, that reality paled by comparison. *Pegasus* hummed around him, her systems running smoothly, somewhere toward the end of her long hyperspace jump.

McCade swung his feet over the side of his bunk and held his head in both hands. It hurt. This was the fourth bracelet-induced dream. God help him if there was a fifth.

In the first dream he'd been an Ilwid, an uninitiated male, living with his sept in a series of underground caverns. As such he'd learned many things, including a respect for his elders, the importance of hard work, and the value of water.

In the second dream he was an Ilwig, a warrior candidate undergoing the rites of malehood, spending twenty day cycles in the desert alone. During his wanderings he'd killed an Ikk, watered himself with its blood, and stumbled across a sacred chamber.

Everyone knew about the sacred chambers the old ones had left behind, but few were lucky enough to see one, much less bear the eternal honor of finding one. Once, the chamber had been filled with wonders, but all had crumbled to dust by the time he found it, all that is except the bracelet.

It was still intact, its single blue-green stone glowing with internal light, its smooth metal warm to the touch.

He knew the bracelet was something special from the moment he slipped it on. A tremendous peace rose to fill his spirit, strange new ideas filled his mind, and his body trembled with excitement.

Through the bracelet he learned that he was the chosen one, that he must lead a life of flawless purity, and that one day his teachings would spread to the stars above.

In the third dream he was an Ilwik, a revered teacher, sought out and honored for his wisdom.

McCade also learned that while almost all Il Ronnian males advance to Ilwig, perhaps one in a thousand goes on to become an Ilwik, or warrior-priest, and of these only a handful are called "great."

He learned that the Ilwik were the leaders of Il Ronnian society. The most senior Ilwik sit on the Council of One Thousand that governs the Il Ronnian homeworld and the empire as well.

The lesser Ilwik run local governments, perform scientific research, teach at universities, lead the armed forces, and perform a hundred other important tasks.

But that was later. McCade would eventually learn that many others had worn the bracelet after the great Ilwik's death, giving it knowledge of recent times, knowledge it had passed along to him.

In the great Ilwik's day the Il Ronnian people had only recently graduated from a hunting-gathering society organized along tribal lines to a slightly more sophisticated social structure, incorporating some rudimentary specialization, but still dependent on subsistence farming.

Among the areas of emerging specialization were farming, metal working, and the priesthood. So it was that the great Ilwik shunned worldly ways and chose to live in a cave that the holy fluid had carved from solid rock eons before.

By late afternoon each day the sun would disappear beyond the rim of the canyon, throwing dark shadows into the valley below. As the heat gradually died away, he'd come forth to meditate, and as their first work came to an end, his brethren would join him. They would arrive by ones and twos, find seats, and wait to receive what he had to give.

Sometimes he spoke, telling them what he knew, and sometimes he remained silent, losing himself in the cosmic flow, inviting them to feel that which can't be said.

And then as the sun began to set, and second work began, they would seek his blessing. Sometimes a blessing was his to give, and he would heal the sick, and sometimes his touch brought only comfort. Either way his brethren gave thanks, paid him honor, and left the gifts of life.

In the fourth dream they killed him. Jealous of his powers his fellow Ilwiks denounced him and presided over his death. They stripped the flesh from his body inch by bloody inch, chanting their empty prayers and capturing his tears in a vial of beautiful crystal. Over and over they ordered him to recant his teachings, and over and over he refused.

So when death finally came it was a release, a gift from God that he gladly accepted. It was from that death that McCade had come, his body drenched with sweat, nerves still tingling from the pain.

Were the dreams true? Was he reliving the actual experiences of an Il Ronnian messiah? It seemed hard to believe, but the dreams were too real, too vivid, to be easily dismissed.

And what about the bracelet? Was it the same one the Il Ronnian teacher had worn? Perhaps so, because the Il Ronn had sent the bracelet and instructed that it be worn.

They'd neglected to mention that once he put the bracelet on, it wouldn't come off. He tried everything short of a cutting torch, and no matter what he did, the bracelet wouldn't budge.

Logic told him the bracelet was an artifact, an ancient device left behind by the same race who had extracted crystals from the mines of Molaria and left enigmatic ruins on a dozen other planets. If so, it might be some sort of recording device, capable of storing memories and transferring them to someone else. Perhaps the messiah had picked the bracelet up, worn it, and in so doing unknowingly recorded his life for others to share.

That would explain the dreams, but it wouldn't explain their content. Why *those* particular dreams in *that* particular order? Surely an ancient machine would transfer memories serially, or even randomly, but this one did neither. There were huge chunks of time missing between the dreams, yet each dream did an excellent job of summarizing a period in the Ilwik's life, and taken together they told his entire life story. Surely that was no accident.

McCade had even wondered if the bracelet was alive, a sentient being of some kind, with its own hidden motives. While he'd never heard of such a life form, it could still exist. After all, he'd encountered a Treel once and seen it take the shape of a woman. But Naval Intelligence had run the bracelet through every test known to man and pronounced it inert.

Of course, what did *they* know? They were safe and sound on Terra, while he ran around Il Ronnian space with a bracelet that wouldn't come off, and someone else's memories doing a tap dance in his head. Assholes.

McCade stood, took two pain tabs, and stepped into the fresher. The hot shower felt good. He blew himself dry and headed for the tiny lounge. He didn't bother to dress since there was no one else on board.

As McCade plopped into a chair he felt something poke him in the right buttock. Reaching down between the cushions, he pulled out one of Molly's toys. A model of *Pegasus* that Phil had made for her.

The toy had a slim, fast look like the ship herself. A one-time navy scout converted to a yacht. He placed it on a shelf and felt a magnet lock it into place.

He wondered where Sara and Molly were, and what they were doing. Swanson-Pierce had promised to take them home, so maybe they were on Alice by now, preparing for another hard winter. He didn't love Alice the way Sara did, but she lived there and that made it home.

And that's why he'd find the Vial of Tears and return it to the Il Ronn. Not for the Empire, not for Swanson-Pierce, but for Sara. For his family. Because if he didn't, the Il Ronnians would come looking for it, and the first battles would be fought out along the rim, over and around planets like his.

And according to Swanson-Pierce, the Il Ronn stood a good chance of winning. Years of budget cutbacks had weakened the Empire's navy, and it would take time to gather what ships there were and shape them into a cohesive force.

So it was his job to find the vial and get it back. And barring that, he'd use up as much time as possible, time the Empire would use to prepare.

Getting the vial back from the pirates would be hard enough, but the Il Ronnians had imposed some conditions as well.

Only one human would be allowed to search for the vial, and first that human must pass the initiations of the Ilwig, or warrior-priest. None other could be allowed to find and touch the sacred relic. It was a frustrating waste of time, but, like it or not, one he'd have to accept.

That was the bad news. The good news was his bounty, the price the Imperial Government had agreed to pay for his services.

The truth was that he'd have done it for free, but they didn't know that, and he felt honor bound to gouge them if he could. It was his form of revenge, his way of getting back at them for the court martial and the years of hardship that followed.

That's why he'd specified five million credits, more money than he could spend, but the exact price of the new hospital Sara wanted. For years the citizens of Alice had been in need of a good medical facility and now they'd have it.

He lit a cigar and activated a viewscreen. What he saw was a computer simulation of what the stars would look like if he and *Pegasus* were travelling in normal space. Real or not they were pretty, glittering like diamonds thrown on black velvet, each one an unfathomable mystery.

Four

HUNDREDS OF RED, yellow, and green eyes stared out at McCade from their electronic lairs. He blew smoke at them and waited for something to happen. *Pegasus* was about to make a hyperspace jump, and as usual, there was little for him to do but wait. *Pegasus* would leave hyperspace in a few moments at the precise point specified by the Il Ronnians.

While routine in toward the center of the human empire, hyperspace jumps were a little more exciting when you were deep inside Il Ronnian space and dependent on *their* coordinates. What if they'd given him the coordinates for a sun? Or a planet? He'd be dead, that's what.

But why bother? There're lots of easier ways to kill a single human.

Nonetheless there was a rock in his gut as the ship's computer made the shift to normal space. The viewscreens shimmered as they switched from simulated to actual input. He felt slightly nauseated but the sensation quickly passed.

Suddenly a host of proximity alarms went off. Someone was waiting for him. A lot of someones. It looked like half the Il Ronnian fleet had turned out to greet him. Battle-ships, cruisers, destroyers, and hundreds of interceptors all swarmed around his tiny ship.

The Il Ronn had been afraid that the treacherous humans might send an entire fleet instead of a single ship. And McCade couldn't blame them. After all, why trust the same folks who ripped you off in the first place?

The dulcet tones of the ship's computer suddenly flooded the control room. It had analyzed the situation and given itself permission to speak. "Due to this ship's current tactical situation, the chances of a successful engagement are zero. Under these conditions any decision to engage will nullify the hull warranty and the manufacturer's responsibility to honor it. If you prefer suicide to surrender, I will dump the ship's atmosphere."

"Gee thanks," McCade replied dryly. "But in this case I think I'll surrender. Now shut up."

Clearly disappointed, the computer snapped, "Have it your way," and returned to its regular duties.

The com set chimed and McCade flicked it on. "Sam McCade."

As the com set came to life McCade found himself face to face with an Il Ronnian naval officer. Although he'd dealt with Il Ronnians before, including a rather unpleasant naval commander named Reez, it was still a shock.

Like all Il Ronnians this one looked like the traditional human image of the "Devil." The alien's eyes were almost invisible under a craggy brow, long pointy ears lay flat against his head, and his leathery skin had a slightly reddish hue. He even had a long tail with a triangular appendage on the end. And McCade knew that down below the range of the vid pickup, there would be two cloven hooves. Everything in fact except horns.

The similarity between Il Ronnian physiology and the traditional Judeo-Christian image of evil had long been a matter for academic debate. Some scholars thought the Il Ronnians' devillike appearance could account for the instant enmity that had sprung up between the two races at first contact. They suggested that after a thousand years of negative conditioning humans weren't capable of liking a race that resembled the devil.

This argument was very popular with those who opposed war with the Il Ronn.

Meanwhile, other scholars disagreed. They maintained that ancient depictions of the devil were based on early visits to Earth by Il Ronnian explorers. Explorers so brutal that their very appearance had come to symbolize evil.

They pointed out that the Il Ronnians had a stardrive long before man, were known to use brutal tactics on less advanced races, and *were* evil.

As a result this second group of scholars felt war was inevitable, and felt the human race might as well get it over with.

Whatever the truth of the matter this Il Ronnian seemed no friendlier than the others McCade had met. His tail twitched back and forth behind his head and he wore a thin-lipped scowl. He spoke flawless Standard like most Il Ronnians of his rank. "I am Star Sept Sector Commander Ceel. You will kill your drives and allow us to take you aboard."

McCade tried for a nonchalant smile. "Valet parking, how thoughtful."

Ceel's scowl deepened and the com set dumped to black.

McCade smiled as he killed his drives. Tractor beams lashed out shortly thereafter to lock *Pegasus* in a powerful embrace and pull her toward a huge battleship.

The ship was miles long and roughly triangular in shape. Designed for travel in deep space, it had none of the aerodynamic smoothness common to smaller ships. An endless array of weapons blisters, solar collectors, cooling fins, and communications antennas covered almost every square inch of the ship's hull. *Pegasus* seemed like a toy as she was pulled into an enormous launching bay and gently lowered into an empty berth.

The outer hatch closed and a thin atmosphere was pumped into the launching bay. This was a sign of his importance, although McCade didn't realize it.

The bay was kept unpressurized most of the time for the convenience of the shuttles and interceptors that constantly came and went. But when important visitors came aboard it was customary to pressurize the bay, saving them the discomfort of wearing space armor.

Of course, outside of his space armor McCade would be more vulnerable, and that too could have played a part in their decision.

A soft chime told him someone was at the main lock. Punching up a surveillance camera, he saw that an entire squad of Il Ronnian Sand Sept troopers stood waiting outside. They were heavily armed.

He activated the intercom. "Hi, guys. Are twelve enough? Maybe you'd better send for reinforcements . . . I'm real grumpy today."

Either the troopers didn't understand him or chose to ignore him, because their stony expressions remained unchanged.

Knowing what to expect, McCade changed into summer-weight trousers and a short-sleeved mesh shirt. Just for the fun of it he strapped on his sidearm as well. It didn't mean much since he was outnumbered a thousand to one, but he was used to wearing one, and the weight of it made him feel better.

He took one last look around to make sure all the ship's systems were powered down, grabbed a fistful of cigars, and headed for the lock.

He cycled through, stepped out onto a set of rollaway stairs, and grinned. Twelve pairs of eyes went to his handgun and back to his face. To his surprise they made no attempt to take it away.

An Eighth Sept Commander stepped forward, cleared his throat nervously, and said, "Star Sept Sector Commander Ceel bids you welcome. Please follow me."

McCade did as he was told. His honor guard, with the emphasis on *guard*, followed along behind. As they marched their steel-capped hooves crashed to the deck in perfect cadence.

They cycled through one of the many locks providing access to the interior of the ship. After the pleasant coolness of the launching bay, it was like stepping into the center of a blast furnace.

Having been on an Il Ronnian ship once before, McCade had prepared himself for the heat but was still surprised by the intensity of it. The Il Ronnians liked to keep their ships warm like the desert planet they came from, and that's why McCade had worn the lightweight clothing, and was soon soaked with his own sweat in spite of it.

The ship was so huge that it took a full fifteen minutes to reach their destination. They marched down sandy brown corridors, rode up lift tubes large enough to accommodate a quarter sept, and rode the rest of the way in a pneumatic tube system.

Wherever McCade went members of the ship's crew stopped to stare. Many had never seen a human before, and those who had were still surprised to see one inside an Il Ronnian warship.

And while McCade had dealt with many alien cultures over the years, he couldn't remember a time when he'd been so completely immersed in one without so much as a single human face to keep him company. It made him feel like a freak, a curiosity led about on a leash, and he didn't like it.

Unlike humans who constantly sought ways to create open spaces in their ships, the Il Ronn preferred the coziness of their traditional underground dwellings, and built their spacecraft accordingly.

So the approach to Sector Commander Ceel's quarters was small and narrow, suddenly opening up into a circular space similar to an underground cave.

As McCade followed the Il Ronnian officer through the passageway, he realized it would force intruders to attack one at a time, giving the defenders one hell of an advantage. A sensible precaution that had found its way from caves to spaceships. As he stepped inside the air crackled around him.

A sensurround gave McCade the impression that he was standing in the middle of a desert. It stretched away in every direction, reddish streaks hinting at a time when the Il Ronnians' skin color had served as protective coloration, finally blending into a purplish sky on the far horizon. Some very real sand crunched under McCade's boots and added to the overall reality of the scene.

He wondered what happened to the sand during zero G maneuvers. Did they vacuum it up or something? There was no way to tell.

Ten Il Ronnians sat in a semicircle before him. They seemed to be sitting on a bench of native stone but appearances were probably deceiving.

In their view the Il Ronnians outranked him, so in keeping with custom, they remained seated. Sector Commander Ceel was the first to speak.

"Welcome, Sam McCade. I see you come before us armed."

McCade tilted his head backward, exposing the major veins in his neck. "A warrior is always armed in defense of his people. My life is yours."

It was a calculated move, a traditional saying straight from the messiah's memories, and it got the desired effect. Ceel was caught entirely off guard, as were most of the other Il Ronnians. They looked at one another in amazement. A polite human? Unheard of!

But one Il Ronnian wore the red cloak of the warrior-priest rather than the purple of the Star Sept. And he was not impressed. "Yes, your life *is* ours, human, and to keep it you need more than a passing knowledge of Il Ronnian custom."

The warrior-priest gestured toward the single rock facing the semicircle of Il Ronnians. "Take a seat."

McCade did as he was told. Real or not, the rock was damned hard and slightly pointy. He was in no danger of falling asleep.

The priest spoke again. "I am Teeb the interrogator. Understand from the start that I oppose your admittance to the honored ranks of the Ilwik. But I must bend before the wishes of my peace-loving brethren and will give you every chance. Every chance that time allows. Unfortunately we must accelerate your testing due to the urgent need for action. Under normal circumstances testing takes place over a period of ten year cycles.''

Teeb paused as though giving McCade time to absorb what he'd said. ''There are two levels of testing, an initial phase in which we will determine your worthiness, and if you qualify, a second phase in which you will undergo the three trials of the Ilwik, or warrior-priest. The first phase will start in a moment. You noticed our battle fleet as you came out of hyperspace?''

McCade nodded. ''Yes, holy one. It was hard to miss.''

Teeb's tail appeared over his head, the pointy appendage shading him from the sun. ''Good. The fleet is here for two reasons. The first is to defend against treachery, something we expect from your kind, and the second is to launch a surprise attack against the human empire should you fail the first tests. Shall we begin?''

Five

McCADE TRIED TO remain calm. It wasn't easy. A test? So soon? What if he failed? He imagined a thousand Il Ronnian vessels flashing out of hyperspace, blasting their way through a scattering of navy ships to destroy planet after planet. Thousands, maybe millions, would die, all because he'd failed some stupid test.

Teeb smiled as though reading his thoughts. "Yes, it is a large responsibility, is it not? I hope your superiors chose well, for their sake, as well as yours."

McCade replied with a crooked smile. "We'll soon know, won't we? Let's get on with it."

"My sentiments exactly," Teeb replied. "You are wearing the holy bracelet of Nik. Millions of candidates have worn it before you, including myself many year cycles in the past."

McCade looked at the bracelet in surprise. "This same bracelet?"

Teeb frowned in annoyance. "That is what I said. Those who the bracelet finds worthy are given certain knowledge, knowledge that I am about to test. Do you understand?"

35

Sweat poured off McCade's body. He should have taken some salt tablets but hadn't thought to do so. If the test took very long, he'd pass out from heat prostration. If so, he'd kill as many of them as he could before he went under. Teeb and Sector Commander Ceel would be the first to go.

McCade wiped the sweat off his forehead and swallowed to lubricate his dry throat. "Yeah, I understand. Like I said before, let's get on with it."

Teeb looked at the other Il Ronnians as if checking to make sure that they'd heard McCade's response. "Good. Here is the first question. When the great teacher was still an Ilwid, or uninitiated male, his egg mother taught him a lesson about the holy fluid. What was that lesson?"

McCade's mind was a complete blank. All he could see was hell bombs falling and entire planets erupting into flame.

A slow smile started across Teeb's thin lips at McCade's silence. It was just as he'd predicted. The human could not answer the question and the farce was almost over. He was just about to call the whole thing off when McCade croaked, cleared his throat, and spoke.

One moment there was nothing but death and destruction, and next McCade had been transported back in time, to a planet he'd never seen. And as the words poured out he knew they were right, because he'd been there, and lived the entire incident along with the young messiah.

He'd been playing hide and seek with a young female named Lees. He was small for his age and often excluded from the rough and tumble male games. As a result he was left to play by himself or with females.

He didn't like being left out, but Lees was more fun than the males, most of whom had little or no imagination. They delighted in seeing who could throw rocks the farthest, run the fastest, or lift the most weight.

Lees, meanwhile, created armies for him to lead, wars for him to fight, and entire kingdoms for him to conquer. She also invented games, his favorite being hide and seek, played in the labyrinth of tunnels shared by their sept.

They would play for hours alternating between excruciating suspense and gleeful discovery. Such was the case the day he violated one of the sept's most important taboos.

It happened because he was having such a good time. The feeling had been there for some time, the unmistakable urge to urinate, but that would mean a long trip through the tunnels to the recycling vats, followed by an equally long trip back. By that time Lees might have lost interest in the game, or gone off to do something else. Besides, he'd found a wonderful hiding place and hated to give it up.

He listened carefully. Nothing. Lees was still a long ways off, probing small airshafts and searching the many storage rooms. This particular storage room was fairly spacious, having its own series of mirrors to bring light down from the surface, and the usual dirt floor.

Stepping in between some huge earthenware pots, he opened his shorts and extruded his penis. It felt good to relax his muscles and let the urine flow out. It made a small puddle before disappearing into the greedy soil.

He had just withdrawn his penis when someone grabbed him from behind. It was Weea, his egg mother. She'd come looking for an empty pot and found her son using the holy fluid to water the sterile soil of a storage room.

Without a word she dragged him through tunnels, up a ramp, and out into the hot sun. The fields were small. Each had been wrested from the grasp of the desert by constant toil and the careful application of holy fluid.

One belonged to his father, a stern male of unyielding discipline, and as Weea jerked him along fear grew in his belly. What would his father do? He'd knowingly violated one of the sept's most closely held taboos. Whatever the punishment it would be swift and terrible.

His father looked up at Weea's approach, his eyes lost in the shadow of his supraorbital ridge. His tail came up to shade the back of his head as thick fingers wrapped and unwrapped themselves around the handle of his hoe. "Greetings, Weea. What brings my mate and youngest son out into this heat?"

Weea bowed her respect. "Greetings, Deeg. Your son

asks many questions about male work . . . and wishes to observe your labors.''

Deeg frowned. ''His interest is fitting. But the sun is hot, too hot for one as young as my son, perhaps another time.''

''Your concern for your son's health does you honor, Deeg, but I ask an exception this day, for I believe the experience will teach him much.''

Deeg was puzzled. Weea was rarely this assertive, but when she was, he'd learned to listen, so his tail signaled assent. ''It shall be as you request. Come over here, son, and sit down on that boundary rock. Watch, and you will learn of male work.''

For the next four hours he watched his father work. Watched as his father broke the ground with an iron bar, watched as he placed each seed into the thin soil by hand, and watched as he watered each seed with the holy fluid.

The merciless sun beat down all the while, leeching every bit of moisture from his skin, heating the rock until he could no longer bear to sit on it.

Finally, after what seemed like an eternity, first work was over and his father led him from the fields.

Nothing more was ever said to him regarding the importance of the holy fluid. There was no need. He'd seen his father work, felt the searing heat of the sun, and understood what Weea wanted him to learn. To waste water was to waste life itself.

As the memory faded away McCade found himself looking at Teeb. The alien's eyes glowed and his voice was tight with anger.

''This proves nothing. The story is a famous one often told to Il Ronnian children. Who knows how the humans learned of it, but it makes little difference since he will fail the next test.''

McCade thought the others looked doubtful, but being no expert on Il Ronnian facial expressions, he couldn't be sure.

''The candidate has passed the first test,'' Teeb said

grudgingly. "Two more await him prior to acceptance. Is the candidate ready?"

McCade tried to concentrate, but he was dizzy, and Teeb's words seemed to come from far, far away. It was hot, so very hot. He heard himself croak something in reply, and did his best to listen as Teeb asked the next question.

"It is known that the great one went forth as an Ilwig to test himself in the desert. While there he found the bracelet you now wear, but he found something else as well, something he later claimed was even more important. What was it?"

Teeb's voice seemed to echo off into the distance and McCade spoke without knowing that he did so. He felt the bracelet on his wrist, a warm and glowing presence, anticipating the excitement it would generate when he came home. But that would have to wait since three day-cycles remained before he could return.

Always hungry, he decided to test his skill as a hunter, and approached a lonely water hole. Like most water holes this one was a sometimes thing, here briefly during the spring, quickly sinking out of sight as the hot hand of summer gripped the land.

A thousand tracks crisscrossed the sands leading up to the water hole. And when the muddy little depression came into sight, he knew he'd see the vicious Ikk drinking side by side with the gentle Vidd. Such was the power of the holy fluid. All creatures needed its essence and must trust their enemies in order to get it.

The sun beat down on his shoulders as he climbed the sandy slope, his broad platelike hooves floating on top of the sand rather than sinking into it, his tail hovering behind his head. Just short of the rim he dropped to hands and knees and crawled the rest of the way.

Peeking over the edge, he saw the usual assemblage of animals, all lapping at the muddy water, all keeping a wary eye on one another. Many of them were good game animals and if he could get closer would fall easily to his spear.

He knew from experience however that the moment he

appeared they would run in the opposite direction, never allowing him close enough for a kill. Still, they were packed so close together that a spear thrown far enough was almost certain to bring one down.

He slid backward down the slope until he could stand without being seen. He withdrew the short spear-thrower from its sheath, fitted the butt of his spear into its socket, and assumed the correct position. It was hard to run uphill and launch the spear at the same time, but he did so, the extra leverage provided by the thrower hurling the spear high into the air. For a moment it was a short black line against the lavender sky. Then it fell straight downward and disappeared beyond the rim of sand.

He ran to the top of the slope and looked. All sorts of animals hopped, scurried, and ran in the opposite direction, leaving one of their number pinned to the sand. He was jubilant at first. His idea had worked!

As he bounded down the slope he screamed his victory for the heavens to hear and waved his spear-launcher over his head. And then he stopped, for he had seen his spear, and the life it had taken.

The Fueek was the most beautiful of all the desert birds, a pink vision against the violet sky, its wings beating with the same rhythm as the Ilwig's heart. And now it was dying, its head jerking pathetically, its beautiful wings beating feebly against the sand.

Unable to give life, he took it, and threw himself down beside the Fueek's body, begging for its forgiveness, as his tears mingled with the bird's blood.

And in that moment he learned many lessons. He learned that each life has its own special value, that random violence is not a tool of the sane, and that the price of sentience is responsibility for one's actions.

This time total silence filled the room as McCade's story came to an end. Slowly, one by one, all heads turned toward Teeb. His head was bent, his eyes on his lap. For a long moment he was perfectly still. When he looked up, McCade saw tears running down his cheeks, and when he spoke, there was wonder in his voice.

"It is true just as the human told it. I am awed and humbled at the power of the great Ilwik. His teachings are so powerful that even a human can understand them. The candidate has passed the second test. One more awaits him prior to acceptance. Is the candidate ready?"

McCade was burning up. He knew he should pull the handgun and kill them, but feared he didn't have the strength to do it. He wavered and almost fell off the rock. He felt his lips crack as he spoke. "I'm ready."

Teeb seemed almost sympathetic as he asked the last question. "I can see that our heat troubles you. I am sorry tradition does not allow a rest period, but your ordeal is almost over.

"Toward the end of the Ilwik's life a great drought came upon the land. The water holes soon dried up, and before long, even the deepest wells began to fail. The crops withered, the animals of the desert disappeared, and soon his people began to die. Saying that 'to understand a problem you must journey to its heart,' the great Ilwik went into the desert alone. What happened then?"

McCade found himself transported into the past once again, placing one weary hoof in front of the other, a lonely figure in the middle of endless desert. For five day cycles he marched out into the desert, and for five day cycles he prayed, until so exhausted he could go no farther. Falling to his knees, he cried out in his agony, "Please, God, we need the boon of your holy fluid to live. Surely you did not make us for the purpose of dying. Where *is* the water we need so badly?"

And suddenly he was someone else, a tall, thin being with long, thin legs that kicked strongly and propelled him forward. It was a strange sensation like flying might be if air were liquid and terribly cold.

Liquid! He was suspended in liquid, not just any liquid, but the holy fluid! This was no vision sent by God, but a horrible profanity, sent up from some dark corner of his soul. What greater waste could there be than to immerse one's body in holy fluid?

But wait, what was that on his long, spindly arm? A bracelet. The same bracelet he'd found in the sacred chamber? It certainly looked the same. If so, this might be part of the bracelet's magic, a memory from its previous owner, a memory called forth by his desperate need for water. Maybe there was meaning here, something he could learn to help his people.

Looking around, he saw there were others like himself in the water, splashing and calling out to one another. No wonder they treated the holy fluid with such casual disregard. They were swimming toward the edge of a huge vat of it, more holy fluid than he'd ever seen, and more than his people could use in years. But where was this liquid treasure?

His host turned to float on his back, allowing him to see a rock ceiling far overhead. So wherever the water was, it was far underground and safe from the sun's hot breath.

It was also cold, colder than anything he'd ever known, so he was joyful when his host turned and headed for shore.

His feet soon found bottom and walked up onto a sandy beach. Picking up a long white cloth he wrapped it around himself and fastened it in place with a large brooch.

A large blue-green stone was set into the very center of the brooch, and the Ilwik noticed it was a perfect match for the one in his bracelet. What had happened, he wondered, that the bracelet was there for him to find and the brooch wasn't? Did the brooch have magic powers as well?

But he never learned the answer because the ancient slipped on some sandals, stepped onto some sort of platform, and floated upward. The ancient stepped off as soon as the platform came to a stop, touched a panel of light, and waited while a heavy door slid open.

As the ancient stepped outside he somehow knew that his host hated the heat and regretted the need to pass through it. And because of that the ancient hurried, not giving the

Ilwik a chance to look around or see where the holy fluid might be.

Up ahead he saw a construction of shining metal, enough metal to make a million spearheads, and it was toward this metal that the ancient carried him. A hole opened in the metal as if by magic and the ancient stepped into the coolness within.

Taking a seat on something shamefully soft, the ancient picked up a large bowl and put it on his head. Much to the Ilwik's surprise he found he could still see as the ancient reached out to touch one of the many lights that glowed before him. It was then that solid metal came to life and vibrated with hidden vitality.

The ancient touched another light and suddenly the Ilwik could see for miles around. There were the three mountain peaks called the "Fingers of Zeek," the long narrow valley called "the place where sun shines not," and stretched out before him the desert called "the land of bones."

He felt the metal lift under him and his spirits soared with it. He knew exactly where he was! Where the holy fluid was! Where his people would come to survive!

And survive they did. Most anyway, though many died on the long trek through the desert and in the mountains beyond. But eventually they found the great reservoirs of the ancients, and the mighty subsurface rivers that fed them, prospering and growing until their eggs hatched in the sands of other planets.

McCade opened his eyes as he croaked out the final words, saw Teeb start to say something, and fell face downward into the hot sand.

Six

"DRINK THIS."

McCade opened his eyes and found himself looking up at the ugliest Il Ronnian he'd ever seen. He'd never seen a really good-looking Il Ronnian, of course, but even by their standards, this one put the ug in ugly. He had a bulging forehead and one eye that was slightly higher than the other.

But the Il Ronnian held a cup of water in one taloned hand and McCade was extremely thirsty. Thirsty enough to accept water from the devil himself.

McCade propped himself up on one elbow and drank greedily.

The Il Ronnian shook his head in mock dismay. "Teeb would have a heart attack if he saw you sucking H_2O like an Ikk at a water hole. You must drink the holy fluid reverently like this."

The Il Ronnian used both hands to pick up a cup of water. Then he bowed his head over it, closed his eyes, and said, "Let life flow through me." Opening his eyes, he drank the water in a series of small sips.

McCade put his cup down and swung his feet over the

side of his bunk. Cool air flowed around him. He was back aboard *Pegasus*.

"Take it easy," the Il Ronnian advised. "You're still suffering from the aftereffects of heat prostration. Since we're a bit short of human doctors, we asked your computer for a course of treatment."

McCade rubbed the back of his neck. "And?"

The alien grinned. "Your computer suggested we put a bullet between your eyes. Do all your computers joke around like that?"

"What makes you think it was joking?" McCade asked.

He got up, groped his way to the medicine cabinet, and fumbled two pain tabs into the palm of his hand. It seemed as if pain tabs were becoming a regular part of his diet. He dumped them into his mouth, squirted some water into a glass, and lifted it to his lips.

Finding the Il Ronnian's eyes on him, he dropped his head, mumbled "Let life flow through me," and gulped the water down.

The Il Ronnian shook his head sadly as he cranked up the gain on his heat cape. "Better . . . but still something short of civilized."

McCade padded down the corridor into the lounge and collapsed into a seat. The Il Ronnian did likewise, his red cape swirling around him.

McCade opened a humidor, took out a cigar, and puffed it into life. His throat felt raw, but he sucked the smoke into his lungs anyway, and blew it out in a long gray stream. He eyed his companion through the smoke. "I don't want to seem ungrateful, but what the hell's going on, and who the hell are you?"

The Il Ronnian smiled. "I'll take your questions in reverse order if you don't mind. My name is Neem, I'm your nif, or tutor. You are an Ilwig, the first human to ever achieve that honor, and you're getting ready for phase two of your testing."

"I passed phase one then?"

Neem nodded. "With flying colors. You really shook

'em up. Up till now everyone had assumed that the bracelet spoke only to Il Ronnians. A bit ethnocentric . . . but understandable nonetheless.''

McCade looked at his wrist. The bracelet was missing.

"It came off when you fell," Neem said in reply to his unasked question.

"That's strange," McCade said, rubbing his wrist. "The damned thing wouldn't budge when I *tried* to take it off."

"I had the same problem," Neem agreed. "But it came off quite easily once my testing was over. Our more rational theologians think the bracelet is some sort of artificial intelligence device that knows that it's become part of our religion and goes along with the gag."

Neem shrugged. "Nonetheless, we continue to take it quite seriously. In fact, if someone else heard you call the bracelet a 'damned thing,' they'd shove a stake up your anus and leave you in the desert to die."

"Sorry," McCade said humbly. "I didn't mean it that way. It's an amazing artifact. I wish my race had one."

Neem gave a very human shrug. "Why? In spite of the bracelet we killed our greatest teachers, including the great Ilwik, and continue to ignore most of his teachings. Wonderful though it is, the bracelet cannot bestow wisdom on those who haven't earned it."

McCade tapped some ash into an ashtray and regarded the Il Ronnian anew. There was something different about him. Where most Il Ronnians were rigidly formal, he was informal. Where most Il Ronnians were distant, he was friendly. And where most Il Ronnians were secretive, he was open. In fact, now that he thought about it, Neem seemed more human that Il Ronnian. Even his manner of speech was more human than Il Ronnian.

McCade pointed his cigar in Neem's direction. "No offense, but you strike me as different somehow, more like a member of my race than yours."

Neem smiled and revealed some razor-sharp dentition in the process. "True. I wondered when you'd notice. As it happens, I'm an expert on human culture; in fact, I have the equivalent of a Doctorate in exoanthropology. Added to that is the fact is that I'm not exactly normal.''

"Not exactly normal?" McCade asked. "In what way?"

"Well," Neem replied, looking down at his lap. "I'm insane.''

McCade choked on some cigar smoke. "Insane? They gave me an insane tutor?"

Neem held up both hands in protest. "It's not as bad as it sounds, Sam. I'm not psychotic or anything. It's just that I'm excessively individualistic. That coupled with an unhealthy interest in humans renders me clinically insane. That's why they made me your nif, because a computer search found that I'm one of the few Il Ronnians who like humans enough to tutor one. Have you noticed how ugly I am?''

McCade tried to look surprised. "Ugly? You look fine to me.''

Neem shook his head. "Nice try, Sam, but among other things, I'm an expert at human facial expressions. The point is that I look like this because of a birth defect. Like the deformed members of most cultures, I was excluded by my peer group throughout childhood and left to my own devices. As a result I was poorly socialized, developed a rather rich fantasy life, and eventually went off the deep end. Or so my shrink says.''

McCade raised an eyebrow. "And what do you say?"

Neem grinned. "I say exactly what any insane person would say. I'm fine . . . and everyone else is crazy.'' Then Neem leaned forward as if sharing a secret.

"Actually this could be my big break. Hanging out with a human is pretty weird, but it sure beats hell out of a rubber room, and if I do well, maybe they'll let me teach again.''

McCade took a deep drag on his cigar and did his best to look sympathetic. Just his luck. An impossible mission, a bizarre initiation into an alien religion, and an insane tutor. What next?

Seven

THE IL RONNIAN homeworld was called Imantha, or "home of the people," and was quite beautiful according to Neem. McCade had to take his word for it because the shuttle put them down on the planet's dark side where he was whisked underground.

While this struck McCade as an unusual time to arrive, Neem assured him it wasn't, pointing out that his people had always been partially nocturnal, and when technology freed them from tending crops during the day, they had become even more so. Now hardly anyone ventured out onto the planet's surface during midday unless forced to do so.

Technology had also allowed the Il Ronn to greatly extend their ancient system of caves and tunnels into a huge network of cities that underlay the surface of Imantha.

One thing hadn't changed though, and that was the Il Ronnian love of warmth. Even though Neem had provided him with a cool suit, McCade's head was still exposed and it was damned hot.

Neem provided a running commentary as a series of anti-grav platforms carried them downward. It seemed the levels nearest the surface were taken up with tightly packed technology. Mines, processing plants, factories, hydroponic farms, defense installations, communications equipment, and more.

Next came the governmental levels where the Council of One Thousand met, and the great septs held their annual conclaves. And below those came the shopping plazas, vast open spaces where the septs hawked their wares, and the residential levels where most of the population lived. An arrangement that also placed the bulk of population deep underground and safe from attack.

It was there that the platform stopped and they got off. Eight Sand Sept troopers went with them.

Neem pulled him into a side passageway after a short walk down a gleaming tunnel. As McCade stepped out onto a small balcony the troopers took up positions outside. A series of lights popped on and a flock of globular vid cams swooped in to hover around him as his eyes fought the sudden glare.

As his eyes adjusted to the light McCade found himself looking down at a hundred thousand Il Ronnians. Even though Neem had warned him what to expect, it was still a disconcerting experience.

The hall was huge and roughly rectangular. McCade saw an endless sea of Il Ronnian faces as he looked down its length. As he bowed the traditional greeting four huge McCades did likewise on wall-sized vid screens. The crowd hissed its approval.

Even though Neem had assured him that Il Ronnian hissing was equivalent to human applause, it still sounded like an army of snakes preparing to strike and made his hair stand on end.

A male voice began to speak in Il Ronnian, and McCade knew that millions, maybe even billions, of Il Ronnians were looking at him on vid screens and holo tanks all over the planet. Much as he detested the whole thing, Neem insisted it was a matter of political and religious necessity.

McCade was coming to understand that Il Ronnian politics were a good deal more complicated than they appeared at first glance.

It seemed that the Council of One Thousand was split into two groups. The conservatives, who tended to be younger and more aggressive, favored a surprise attack on the Empire. The liberals meanwhile were generally older and more experienced, and wanted to give the humans a chance to recover the vial themselves.

The liberals had sponsored this public appearance in an effort to sway public opinion, an important factor in a society governed by mutual consensus.

While the Il Ronnian public was understandably upset about the loss of the holy relic, they were also curious about the human who had promised to find it and were eager to learn more about him. So the liberals hoped McCade would make a good impression and buy them some time.

He knew the Il Ronnian voice was introducing him, telling the public that he'd already passed the first phase of testing, and inviting them to witness phase two. It seemed there were plans to televise his activities from this point on. Neem said this would serve to build liberal support and provide the population with some free entertainment to boot.

"But what if I fail?" McCade had asked.

"Then the conservatives will get their way and attack," Neem had replied with a characteristic shrug. "And since I'm certifiably insane, they'll make me a full Sector Commander."

McCade saw very little humor in the Il Ronnian's joke considering the implications for the human empire.

McCade felt Neem jab him in the back as the Il Ronnian voice stopped. It was his turn to speak. His words had been carefully rehearsed during the trip to Imantha, and computer-checked to make sure the translation from human Standard to Il Ronnian wouldn't introduce any inaccuracies. As he spoke an Il Ronnian translator would echo his words a fraction of a second later.

"I bring greetings from my people to yours. It is a privilege to visit your home planet, to undergo the trials of the Ilwik, and to speak to you this night.''

The crowd swirled slightly and a great hissing filled the air. McCade waited for it to die down. ''Thank you. There has long been tension between our two races as is natural when two great empires come together and almost touch. And where we come together sparks sometimes fly, lives are tragically lost, and neither race profits. Such was the case when some humans raided the planet you call Fema and took the holy Vial of Tears.''

At the mention of the holy relic a deep growling filled the air, and sweat popped out on McCade's forehead as he found himself looking down at one hundred thousand devils, each one voicing his or her hatred. He swallowed dryly as the noise died away.

''Yes, I understand your anger, and ask you to understand that those who took the vial acted on their own without the knowledge and consent of the human Emperor. And, God willing, that's why I will hunt them down and kill them, taking the vial and returning it to the Il Ronnian people.''

Now the hissing became a sibilant roar, as thousands of tails lashed their approval, and the crowd surged forward in its excitement.

McCade had questioned his last statement, pointing out that he couldn't promise to find the vial, much less kill the people who'd taken it.

But Neem had waved his objections away. He said the statement was simply a sop to the conservative party that shouldn't be taken too seriously. Looking out at the roaring crowd McCade wasn't too sure. They seemed to believe he could do it. How would they react if he failed?

For the hundredth time he cursed the various forces that had conspired to put him where he was, lifted an arm to wave to the crowd, and watched as the four gigantic McCades did likewise.

He waved one last time as he felt Neem tug on the back of his cool suit, glad to have the whole thing over.

As he left the balcony the Sand Sept troopers closed in

around him once more. Together they marched through a series of passageways and down a wide escalator. Additional Sand Sept troopers had been positioned to keep a lane clear for their use.

As he stepped off the bottom of the escalator McCade found himself on a broad platform. Fifty or sixty Il Ronnians were scattered across the platform. Beyond it was a huge tube of some transparent material. He couldn't tell if they'd witnessed his recent performance or not, but they turned to watch him with curious eyes as he arrived.

Moments later there was a soft whooshing sound as an enormous train arrived inside the transparent tube and a series of doors hissed open. It was clearly some sort of underground transcar system, but on a scale McCade had never seen before.

"The second car back is ours," Neem said, "or so I was told. It would seem that you're getting the VIP treatment."

McCade glanced at the Sand Sept troopers and back to Neem. "VIP? What does that stand for, very important prisoner?"

Neem smiled but refused to meet his eyes. "You're not looking at this the right way. The troopers are here to protect you. I'm not the only crazy Il Ronnian on the planet. There're others, some of whom are diehard conservatives and quite violent."

"Thanks," McCade replied dryly. "I feel a lot better now."

Once inside McCade discovered the train was as large as it appeared. While no other passengers had been allowed to board their car, he could tell that it normally held hundreds of riders.

He noticed that the bottom of each seat had a three-inch slot that ran front to back. At first he couldn't figure out what it was for, until he saw Neem take a seat and saw how neatly the Il Ronnian's tail slid back through the slot. Then the tail arched up and over the back of the chair to appear over Neem's shoulder. Now it could become part of the alien's nonverbal communication once again. Later McCade would notice that almost all Il Ronnian chairs featured this same design.

Like everything else the Il Ronnians used, the inside of the train was warm, way too warm. McCade opened the two nozzles located on the chest of the suit and directed the cool air up toward his face. He knew this would put an increased demand on the power pak, but what the heck, he'd just ask Neem for another.

Feeling somewhat better, McCade turned his attention to the large windows that lined both sides of the car. There was nothing much to see. Just solid rock flashing by at incredible speed. Neem volunteered an explanation.

"If you build most of your cities underground, it only makes sense to put your major transportation systems there as well. This particular train runs on the surface for short periods of time, but since it's night up there, you still won't see much."

McCade nodded, kicked his feet up onto the opposite bench, and watched the rock walls flash by until he drifted off to sleep.

"Well, this is it," Neem said cheerfully. "After this morning, phase one of the testing will be out of the way."

"Or I'll be dead," McCade answered as he fastened the last seal on his cool suit. The long train ride had left him tired and grumpy. After the train trip he'd been transferred here, to the Wa'na, or sacred testing grounds.

He was in a rather Spartan dressing room at the moment. The only furnishings consisted of an Il Ronnian water shrine and a table heaped high with weapons. The shrine was a sealed biosphere that depicted a natural spring bubbling up between lichen-covered rocks.

The walls were made of bare durocrete and were completely featureless except for an ominous-looking metal door. When he stepped through it the testing would begin.

Neem had already explained that like the first phase of testing, the second involved three separate tests, each corresponding to one aspect of life. The first, and the one he would tackle today, was the physical. It included athletic ability, the martial arts, and an appreciation of physical beauty.

The second level was mental. It included the ability to reason, academic as well as experiential learning, and the ability to manipulate the environment through use of tools.

The third level was the spiritual, and it involved a mastery of both the first and second levels, but a mastery that incorporated certain concepts. Primary among them was love and compassion.

But love and compassion were far from McCade's mind as he approached the table and eyed the weapons laid out on its surface. He'd been told to expect physical combat, but that's all he knew, and it made the choice a difficult one. After all, depending on who your enemy is, some weapons are more effective than others.

But he'd always found that slug guns serve a variety of needs, so he left the Molg-Sader belted around his waist and checked to make sure that he had two extra magazines.

Of course, energy weapons have advantages too, so McCade hedged his bet and picked up a brand–new blast rifle. He noticed it was marine issue and wondered how it had fallen into Il Ronnian hands. Whatever the answer, he knew he wouldn't like it.

Then he passed a bandolier of energy paks over his head and decided to call it a day. There were lots of other weapons he could have chosen, everything from frag grenades to rocket launchers, but each additional weapon would add weight and slow him down. So if the Il Ronnians had a main battle tank waiting for him out there, he was just plain out of luck.

McCade recognized Teeb's voice as it flooded in over some hidden speaker. "It is time for the candidate to enter the Wa'na. Please enter through the metal door. Good luck, Ilwig McCade."

Much to McCade's surprise, Teeb sounded as if he meant it.

McCade had his hand on the door when he remembered something. Acting on impulse he returned to the water shrine and intoned the traditional prayer. "As you flow through heaven and earth, flow also through me, watering my spirit and making it grow."

As he opened the door and went through he missed Neem's smile and the words that went with it. "Assuming you survive you'll make one hell of an Il Ronnian someday. Good luck!"

Eight

MCCADE SQUINTED INTO bright sunlight. Sheer canyon walls rose on every side exposing layers of sediment stained here and there with streaks of red.

An island of solid rock stood in front of him. It had once forced a mighty river to divide itself in half forming two channels, one right and one left.

The river was gone now, but rocks both large and small remained as silent witnesses to a time when Imantha had been very different. A time when the holy fluid had leaped and splashed its way through the canyon on its journey to a distant sea.

Gravel crunched under McCade's boots as he turned a full circle. He held the blast rifle up and ready. Would his opponent attack without warning? Or would he hear some sort of official statement first?

McCade knew as all bounty hunters did that real violence comes without warning. But when violence has been institutionalized and turned into entertainment, it must be justified and explained for the comfort of those who view it.

The violence might otherwise seem primitive and uncivilized, and that would never do.

Knowing this, McCade smiled as a flight of vid cams appeared overhead and Teeb's voice echoed between the canyon walls. "In a moment the first phase of your testing will begin. As you know the test will measure your ability to deal with the physical world. Violence is a part of the physical world and to recover the Vial of Tears you will be forced to fight many battles. So we will confront you with five armed opponents.

"All are humans captured during a raid on one of our planets. You may deal with them in whatever fashion you think appropriate. All are experienced warriors, all are well armed, and all will go free if they kill you. Do you understand?"

"I don't want to seem ungrateful or anything," McCade said dryly, "but there's no need to be so generous with opponents. Wouldn't one be enough?"

"For most candidates it would be," Teeb replied evenly. "But you are a professional killer. So to ensure a fair contest we gave you five opponents. Do you have any other comments or questions?"

Although he didn't agree with Teeb's description of him as a "professional killer," McCade decided to let it go.

"Nope, I think that about covers it. It's good to know that you're keeping everything fair."

"Very well then. Your opponents have been released about two of your miles down canyon. The rest is up to you."

With that the vid cams darted in every direction and took up new positions that would allow them to cover the action.

McCade began to run. He chose the right channel, dodged between boulders as he searched for a hiding place. Given the odds he'd prefer to hole up somewhere and let them come to him. All he needed was some cover and a rear exit. Unfortunately he didn't see anything that even came close.

He rounded the other end of the island and came to a sudden stop. There was an open stretch up ahead where the two channels came back together, and while some large boulders dotted its surface, they didn't offer much cover.

Beyond that some upthrust rock formations had forced the river to divide once again and form a number of smaller channels. The river was gone but the channels weren't and they formed a natural maze. Not the sort of place where McCade wanted to play hide and seek with five killers.

He turned and ran full speed at the island. As he ran McCade picked a path through the jumble of rocks and headed for the top in a series of long jumps.

From up there he'd be able to see them coming and establish a good angle of fire as well. They'd have him trapped of course, but there's no such thing as a perfect plan.

It wasn't long before the easy jumps gave way to a serious climb. The ancient river had worn the boulders smooth and footholds were hard to come by. For every two feet of progress made, it seemed as if one was lost.

Meanwhile there were five killers headed his way. He wouldn't know they were there until a slug took him between the shoulder blades. He wanted to look but couldn't. Looking would waste precious time.

He told himself that they'd come slowly. They'd be on the lookout for an ambush and their progress would be slowed by the same maze of channels that he'd decided to avoid.

His arguments made sense, but there was still a hard itchy feeling between his shoulder blades as McCade pulled himself over the top and rolled out of sight.

Moving on hands and knees, McCade hid behind a jumble of rocks, unslung the blast rifle, and flipped the sight to high mag. He swept the weapon from left to right and checked for signs of movement.

Except for shimmering heat waves and the occasional bird, everything was still. A Fueek bird flapped its way upward to soar against the violet sky. McCade remembered the great Ilwik's love for Fueek birds and decided that this one was a good omen.

It was suddenly warmer inside his cool suit and McCade turned over to check for damage. Sure enough, there was a four-inch tear just above the right knee. He could feel cool air spilling out when he held his hand over the hole. Damn!

If he tried to repair the tear, his opponents might break into the open when he wasn't looking. And if he didn't repair the tear, he'd run the very real risk of heat prostration.

McCade swore under his breath as he opened a pocket on his left sleeve and withdrew a small patch kit. He tore it open with fumbling fingers and spilled precut patches all over the ground.

Picking up a rectangular patch with one hand he used the other to squeeze bonding material onto its inside surface. The moment the entire thing was covered McCade slapped the patch into place and felt the temperature begin to drop. It worked!

Then he caught movement from the corner of his eye. Two of the hovering vid cams suddenly jumped upward and spun toward the rocky maze. Someone knew something he didn't.

Grabbing his blast rifle, McCade rolled over to peer through the sight. One, two, three, wait a minute, yes, there they were, four and five. The suited figures had just emerged from the maze and were working their way up channel toward the open space. They were out of range, but it gave McCade a chance to check out the opposition.

Number one was a woman. Her shoulder-length black hair swayed around her face as she moved and her weapon was pointed at the ground. She had the point, which suggested a leader, either elected or self-appointed.

But wait a minute. Look at number two. Was he wrong, or was number two's weapon aimed at number one's back? Number two was a hefty man with a large bald spot and a hard face. What was this? Mutiny? Or something else?

McCade swept his sight across the other three. There were two men and a woman. As they advanced they were close enough to communicate but too far apart to nail with a single burst. Very cool, very professional. These people knew what they were doing.

McCade felt the muscle in his left cheek begin to twitch. Okay, three, four, and five were hard bodies who knew one end of a blaster from the other. But what about numbers one and two?

Maybe two was just a wee bit careless about the way he held his weapon, or maybe there had been a falling out among thieves, or maybe number one was being *forced* to take the point. She'd draw the first fire and give the others a chance to find cover. If so, then number two was the leader, and a prime target.

Number one paused at the edge of the open area clearly hesitant to cross it. But number two gave her a shove and she stumbled forward, almost falling before regaining her balance. And number two was right behind her as she ran from one scrap of cover to the next, his weapon centered on her back.

McCade found himself wishing for a cigar and forced the thought away. It was time to reduce the odds a little. He seated the rifle butt against his right shoulder, flicked the safety off, and centered the sight on a patch of open ground.

This particular patch was directly in front of number four's position. In order to reach the next rock four would have to pass through it, and when he did, McCade would nail him.

It would be a simple shot. Energy weapons aren't subject to the effects of wind or gravity as are slug throwers. Of course they don't pack much kinetic energy either, so if you're trying to drop a charging Envo Beast, you might choose something with a little more wallop. But an energy beam does go where you aim it and for this situation the blast rifle was ideal.

Number four took off like a jackrabbit and ran right into the energy beam. It sliced down through his left shoulder and cut diagonally across his chest. The two halves of his body separated in a bright shower of blood.

A vid cam swooped down for a better shot as McCade

turned his attention to number five. Something winked to the right and fire splashed the rock by his head. Number five was shooting back!

McCade rolled left as another energy beam screamed through the space he'd just vacated. Number five was a good shot.

McCade eased the barrel of his weapon through a gap in the rocks, caught a flash of movement, and fired. His energy beam punched a hole through number five's right leg, causing her to stumble and fall.

Using her hands and one good leg, number five managed to drag herself behind a ledge.

McCade let her go. Two down and three to go.

Swinging his weapon left, McCade searched for numbers one and two. He just caught a glimpse of them as they made it to the base of the island. He'd have to stand against the skyline in order to see them and that would provide number three with an opportunity to blow his head off. Where *was* number three anyway?

Conscious that numbers one and two were busily climbing his way, McCade moved to the right. If possible he wanted to find three and deal with him before one and two arrived.

He could feel the seconds ticking away as he quartered the ground below. Each second brought numbers one and two closer and increased the odds against him.

He was just about to give up when he saw a flash of white toward the top of his scope.

McCade tilted the rifle down and found his cross hairs centered on number three's back. The bastard was running away! His finger touched the firing stud and stopped. Later he might regret the decision, but McCade couldn't bring himself to shoot a man in the back.

He turned and was just starting to get up when numbers one and two popped up from behind a jumble of rocks. They were fast!

Something snatched the blast rifle from his hands and McCade dived sideways hoping to ruin their aim.

He hit hard and felt rather than saw the bullets that followed along behind. They spanged off the surrounding rocks as he rolled onto his back and felt the slug gun fill his hand. It came up and he saw a white suit fill his sight.

It was number one! Number two had an arm around one's throat and was using her as a shield! One struggled and two's bullets went wide.

McCade screamed at her. "Drop, damn you, drop!"

Number one dropped. McCade felt the slug gun buck in his hand as she did and saw three red flowers blossom down the front of number two's cool suit. Number two staggered, the slug gun flew from his hand, and he fell over backward into a pool of his own blood.

McCade kept the slug gun centered on number one as he struggled to his feet. He hoped it was over but couldn't be sure. For the first time he noticed that she was very, very pretty, with wide-set brown eyes, a long, straight nose, and a generous mouth.

Her voice trembled when she spoke. "He took the power pak out of my weapon. Are you going to kill me?"

McCade holstered the slug gun and patted his pockets for a cigar. "Not unless you think I should."

She looked at number two and shuddered. "All of them outranked me so they made me take the point." She paused. "They call me Reba. I'm surprised to be alive."

McCade found a broken cigar, stuck it between his teeth, and puffed it into life. "I know what you mean, Reba. So am I."

Nine

McCade was allowed to rest for one rotation before the next test began. He spent some of his time eating and sleeping and the rest being tutored by Neem.

Among other things McCade learned that the Il Ronn had fifteen different words for heat. Each one conveyed a slightly different quality of heat, and was associated with a time of day or a type of activity.

While this kind of complexity made the Il Ronnian language difficult to learn, it also made it extremely precise and a joy to scientists and poets alike.

Though not sure what to do with this sort of information, McCade found it interesting and the time passed quickly. Before he knew it the rest period was over and Teeb was leading the way to the next test site.

The warrior-priest was no longer hostile. If anything, he'd assumed a proprietary air as if McCade were his invention and a rather clever one at that.

Neem trailed along behind, his tail swishing back and forth in amusement. At this rate they'd have to make room for Teeb at the Institute for Mental Rehabilitation. After all, anyone who liked humans *must* be crazy.

Meanwhile, Teeb had continued his conversation with McCade. Although his tone was friendly, the Il Ronnian's eyes glowed like red coals. "Well, human, what did you think of the first test?"

McCade considered his answer carefully before speaking. "As the great Ilwik once said, 'All things are connected.' In retrospect the test was not entirely physical."

"Yes!" Teeb responded eagerly. "*None* of the tests are entirely what they seem. Tell me, *how* did you pass the test?"

McCade had already given the matter some thought so his answer was ready. "I passed because of things I *didn't* do."

Teeb gave McCade a friendly pat on the back. The impact drove him forward a step and a half. "You amaze me, human! You are correct. You passed because you *did not* panic, you *did not* make stupid assumptions, and you *did not* kill unnecessarily. All virtues of the warrior-priest. But best of all you knew *why* you did as you did."

Actually McCade hadn't figured it out until *after* the test, but since Teeb was so pleased, he saw no reason to straighten the alien out.

The corridor was long, tubular, and increasingly busy. Many Il Ronnians stopped to stare as McCade and his entourage passed by.

McCade did his best to ignore them, but found that somewhat difficult when juveniles ran up to pinch him. Most were intercepted by the Sand Sept troopers, but some got through, and it hurt when they pinched him. Fortunately his cool suit absorbed most of the punishment.

Teeb's long red robe made a soft swishing noise as it dragged along the floor. "During your second test you will play a game called 'Encirclement.' It requires a good memory, an agile mind, and other qualities as well."

They paused as the Sand Sept troopers intercepted a flying squad of young Il Ronnians before continuing on their way.

"I want you to know that we have gone to extreme lengths to make the game fair," Teeb said seriously. "Encirclement is something of a passion with many Il Ronnians, and since you have never played before, it took some effort to locate a suitable opponent. I think that is our door just ahead."

The door was one of many that lined the corridor. Each bore a number and some serpentine Il Ronnian script. McCade tried to open it but was brushed aside by a rather large Sand Sept trooper.

Moments later the trooper was back, signaling the all-clear with his tail and holding the door open so they could enter.

McCade followed Teeb into a large circular room. The walls and ceiling radiated a soft violet light, and like every other Il Ronnian room he'd been in, it was hotter than hell.

A beautiful mosaic covered the floor. Thousands, maybe millions, of stone chips had been used to fashion pictures, each beautiful in itself but part of a much larger whole. Darker stones framed the pictures and went together to form a large grid. And when viewed as a whole the grid formed a desert landscape. And the landscape was filled with Il Ronnian birds, animals, and legendary beasts.

McCade noticed that a large number of red rocks had been stacked on one side of the room, while an equal number of green rocks had been piled on the other. The rocks were highly polished and of uniform size and shape.

"Here is your opponent now. Eena, this is the human called McCade."

McCade turned to find himself looking down into the serious face of a young Il Ronnian female. As far as he could tell the only difference between male Il Ronnians and female Il Ronnians were the colorful sashes the females wore over their loose robes. Apparently the Il Ronnians could tell the difference however, since there were plenty of them.

"I hope you will not be offended by the fact that Eena is not an adult, but given Encirclement's popularity, it was difficult to locate a suitable opponent. However, Eena is the best player in her hatching and I think she will offer you a sufficient challenge.''

Although Eena was no more than ten cycles old, and came no higher than his waist, McCade saw her eyes glitter with anticipation. She planned to clean his clock.

McCade bowed his respect. ''Greetings, Eena. May you grow and hatch many eggs.''

Eena bowed in return. She spoke Il Ronnian, but the translator pinned to her robe turned it into flawless Standard. ''Greetings, human. May you eat feces and die an agonizing death.''

McCade looked at Teeb with a raised eyebrow. ''What's the problem? Have I got bad breath or something?''

The warrior-priest grinned his amusement. ''Eena means no disrespect. She is using psychological warfare. She hopes to unnerve you. Such ploys are an accepted part of Encirclement.''

McCade nodded his understanding. ''Fair enough. If you'll explain the rules, shorty and I will get this game off the ground.''

Eena winced at the term ''shorty,'' and McCade grinned. This could be fun.

Teeb cleared his throat importantly. ''Here is how the game of Encirclement is played. You will notice that the floor has been divided into a grid. There are nineteen vertical and nineteen horizontal lines. As a result there are three hundred sixty-one intersections or positions where you can place the stones that are either red or green. Please choose a color.''

McCade looked at the piles of red and green stones and then at Eena. He noticed that her face was carefully neutral. She wanted one color over the other. He took a guess. ''I'll take the red stones.''

Eena's mouth turned down into a scowl. Her red sash had given her away.

''Good,'' Teeb acknowledged, his tail signaling approval. ''The two of you will take turns placing stones, also called warriors, on the intersections where the vertical and horizontal lines meet. Each of you will attempt to encircle as many vacant intersections as possible. When both of you are satisfied that all the potential territory has been taken, you will count the vacant points encircled by your warriors, and subtract the number lost through capture. The individual with the most points wins."

"Capture?" McCade asked. "How does that work?"

"A good question," Teeb answered approvingly. "When two or more of your opponent's warriors occupy adjacent positions on a vertical or horizontal line, they are considered a sept and can be captured when encircled by your stones. As long as one of its members adjoins a vacant intersection the sept is free, but when the sept is completely surrounded, it is taken hostage and removed from the board. Understood?"

"Understood," McCade answered.

"Excellent," Teeb said approvingly. "In that case I'll leave you to it. Have a good match." Teeb's tail waved good-bye as he headed for the door.

Neem sidled up to McCade as Eena went over to inspect her stones. Speaking softly he said, "Don't forget to cheat."

"What?"

Neem looked around nervously and said it again. "I said, don't forget to cheat. I'm an expert on human culture remember?"

"Yeah, so?"

"So many humans disapprove of cheating. We don't. We don't talk about it, but everyone cheats if they can get away with it. So unless you keep an eye on Eena, she'll steal the match out from under you."

McCade nodded thoughtfully. "Thanks, Neem. I'll keep it in mind."

Neem left as a swarm of vid cameras entered and took up positions in various parts of the room.

As one came to hover over his head McCade wondered how many Il Ronnians were watching and whether they were for or against him. According to Neem, McCade had quite a following, liberals mostly, but a scattering of independents as well. Of course, none of them were really rooting for *him*, they were opposed to war and wanted him to succeed for that reason.

"Make your move, human scum."

McCade turned to find Eena scowling up at him. Her attempts to intimidate him were kind of cute. And even though she'd eventually grow up to look like the devil himself, there was something appealing about her pinched little face and big determined eyes.

He patted her shoulder. "Thank you, Eena. You're pretty cute for a short person. I'll grab a rock and be right back."

He headed across the room without waiting for a response and picked up a red rock. For some reason he'd imagined the stones were artificial and therefore lighter than they looked. Nothing could have been further from the truth.

The stones were real and weighed about twenty-five pounds apiece. Later he'd learn that this particular court had been designed for male grand masters. Most courts were a good deal less fancy, and many Il Ronnians preferred to play on miniature boards or computer terminals. But this was a full-blown traditional court complete with real rocks.

McCade carried his stone to the middle of the grid, picked an intersection, and plopped it down.

He saw a look of enormous satisfaction come over Eena's face. The human had placed his first warrior in the middle of the desert! At this rate the ugly alien would beat himself!

Eena selected one of her own stones, struggled to pick it up, and staggered over to the far corner of the grid where she carefully lowered it into place.

The stones were way too heavy for her and McCade was tempted to help. But should he give up an advantage? Perhaps the weight of the stones had been factored into the match as part of her handicap. And what if he *had* to win in order to pass this test? By helping her he might call down a nightmare of destruction on his own kind.

With those thoughts in mind McCade decided to let Eena fend for herself. Meanwhile he'd do his best to win the match.

Having analyzed Eena's last move, McCade realized that the corners of the grid were easier to defend than the middle. Like her he would start in the corners and work his way out.

He selected another stone, placed it in close proximity to Eena's, and stepped back to watch her reaction.

What he got was a look of resignation, as though she'd realized that his stupidity couldn't last forever, and been forced to accept it.

Well, he *thought* it was a look of resignation, but how could he be sure? He'd picked up on some Il Ronnian facial expressions from Neem, but still couldn't tell if Eena was resigned, or just suffering from indigestion. He decided to assume the former and placed another stone near hers.

And so it went stone after stone, intersection after intersection, until McCade was almost completely surrounded. Eena had also captured small contingents of his warriors so now he was outnumbered as well as poorly positioned. He was going to lose, that much was certain.

Nonetheless, McCade was determined to make the best showing he could. So there was only one thing left to do. Follow Neem's advice and cheat.

By now the weight of the stones had started to take their toll on Eena. McCade estimated that each of them had around two hundred stones at their disposal, and at twenty-five pounds apiece, that came to more than two tons of rock.

So each time Eena went for another stone her movements were a little slower, her steps a little more uncertain, and her eyes a little more out of focus.

McCade's heart went out to her, but he steeled himself with visions of what might happen to Molly if he failed the test and set about using Eena's predicament to his advantage.

Usually it was a simple matter of sliding her warriors off one intersection and onto another less important position. And sometimes he moved his own stones, subtly improving their positions and worsening Eena's.

The vid cams swooped and hovered throughout all this, picking up his activities and transmitting them to thousands of Il Ronnians all over the planet. What did they think of his cheating? There was no way to tell.

Eena came close to catching him more than once, returning from the pile of stones to find the board slightly altered, frowning as she tried to remember where all the pieces had been. Had he been a peer, or had she been less exhausted, maybe she would've said something. But she didn't and the game went on.

Time after time she returned to the ever dwindling supply of green stones, and time after time she hauled one back, until it was obvious that she was on the edge of physical collapse. But the little Il Ronnian had guts and refused to give up.

By this time McCade had begun to feel sorry for her. He kept looking up at the hovering vid cams, waiting for Teeb to declare that the game was over, that Eena could stop. But nothing came.

Damn it! Why continue this farce? Eena had won all but a final victory and could hardly keep on her feet.

McCade set about reversing the effects of his cheating. Making almost no effort to conceal his movements, he rearranged Eena's warriors so they surrounded twice the intersections they had before and captured half his remaining warriors in the bargain. Maybe he'd lost the match, maybe he'd failed the test, but he couldn't bear to watch Eena carry more rocks.

Eena finally staggered up with her last stone, dropped it onto an intersection with a heavy thud, and surveyed the grid. Then she realized that her warriors dominated the entire grid and her features lit up with delight. She gave a whoop of joy and her tail stood at attention as she jumped up and down. "I won! I won!"

The vid cameras spun and dipped as they picked up final shots, and McCade wiped the sweat off his forehead with the back of his hand. He looked down at Eena and grinned. "You sure did, shorty. You won fair and square."

Ten

IT SEEMED LIKE a long time before Teeb came. McCade spent it smoking cigar after cigar until his room was thick with dark blue smoke. Finally coughing and hacking, Neem left McCade alone with his own dark thoughts.

Had he passed their stupid test or not? The least the pointy-eared bastards could do was tell him. The whole thing was silly. Yes, he understood how much the sacred vial meant to the Il Ronnian people; yes, he understood that according to tradition only a full Ilwik could undertake a holy quest; yes, he knew what was at stake.

But it wasn't fair. The tests had no clear rules, the odds were stacked against him, and the penalty for failure was way too high.

If he failed, would the Il Ronnian ships really blast out of hyperspace and lay waste to the rim worlds? Was a vial full of liquid really worth an interstellar war? Unfortunately the answer came back "yes," and the knowledge plunged him even deeper into despair.

In typical Il Ronnian fashion Teeb didn't knock when he

entered McCade's room. Instead he barged right in waving some sort of print-out over his head.

"You know what *this* is, human?"

McCade did his best to look bored. "I haven't got the slightest idea."

"It is an audience consensus . . . that is what it is!"

"A consensus?"

"Yes, our society operates on consensus, as you know, and the only way to test consensus is to sample the population on a regular basis. And according to the people you passed the second test by an even larger margin than the first one!"

McCade was suddenly on his feet. "What? You mean *the audience* decides whether I pass or fail?"

Teeb looked momentarily mystified. "Yes, of course. Who else would decide?"

McCade's jaw dropped. "I don't know. I assumed there was a committee or something."

Teeb dismissed the idea with a wave of his tail. "Only humans would let others make such an important decision for them. On Imantha everyone has a say."

A feeling of tremendous relief swept over McCade as he fell back into his chair. He'd passed! Never mind that the whole thing was completely insane, he'd passed!

Teeb paced back and forth, his tail twitching, his eyes glowing with enthusiasm. "What a match! You are without a doubt the worst player in this sector of space! Eena out positioned you from the start, and cheat, my goodness that youngster could cheat!"

"Cheat?" Even though Neem had warned him of the possibility, and even though he'd done it himself, it hadn't occurred to McCade that Eena had cheated too.

Teeb laughed. "Of course. Eena moved your warriors around more than you did!"

McCade felt suddenly defensive. "Well, if I performed so poorly, how come I passed the test?"

Teeb was suddenly serious. "Because you did the best you could in a situation where all the odds were stacked against you, because you managed to adapt to changing circumstances, because you chose to risk all to help the weak.''

McCade was silent for a moment and then he spoke. ''The audience said all that?''

Teeb's tail signaled agreement. ''That is correct, human. The audience said all that.''

McCade nodded soberly. ''I see. So what's next?''

''That,'' Teeb replied with a toothy grin, ''is for me to know, and for you to find out.''

Eleven

THE TRUMPETS MADE a long mournful sound as McCade walked down the broad aisle towards the Rock of Truth. To his right and left ten thousand Il Ronnians stood and bowed their respect. He noticed that most wore the uniform of the Star Sept.

Gravel crunched under his boots and he heard the sound of his own breathing as he walked up a curving path to emerge on top of a flat rock.

It was from this spot that the great Ilwik had ministered to his followers so long ago. As the sun dropped behind the canyon walls they had come forth to hear him speak, and in his latter days trumpets had announced his arrival.

And even though the canyon had been roofed over five hundred cycles before, and its floor made smooth for the comfort of the people, it was the same place. A holy place imbued by time and use with a sense of profound peace and quiet.

A shiver went down McCade's spine as he looked out over the assembled multitude. The usual vid cameras danced here and there as filtered sunlight streamed down from huge

77

skylights and twenty thousand devils waited for him to speak. It couldn't, shouldn't, be happening, yet here he was about to judge and be judged in return. He held up both hands as an audio pickup moved in to hover near his mouth.

"In the name of the great Ilwik I bid you welcome. Please be seated." Thanks to translating devices his voice spoke perfect Il Ronnian as it boomed the length of the canyon.

As the twenty thousand Il Ronnians took their seats they made a loud rustling sound like the wind passing through dry vegetation.

McCade sat on the same rock the Ilwik had favored and pulled out a cigar. The Il Ronn didn't smoke so they had no prohibitions against it. McCade puffed the cigar alight and blew out a column of smoke with his first words.

"My name is Sam McCade. Although I am not an Il Ronnian, I have worn the bracelet and seen through the great Ilwik's eyes. I come before you to judge a crime, and to be judged in return, for if I fail there will be a terrible war. Let us all pray that justice will prevail. The prosecution may begin."

Neem and he had rehearsed everything up to this point, but he'd have to wing it from here on out, and that wouldn't be easy. Ilwiks had dispensed justice at the tribal or sept level of Il Ronnian society in ancient times. But as the need for specialization grew, they had gradually transferred that function to occupational groupings.

So, if a clerk in the Department of Census beat his mate, the matter would be heard by an Ilwik from that same department, and the judgment would be confirmed or modified by a jury of his peers. Il Ronnian theory held that they alone were truly his peers and best able to confirm or deny his punishment.

And according to Neem it wasn't unusual for some cases to be assigned to individuals in the final stages of testing. For in the Il Ronnian view, justice and religion were part and parcel of the same thing. And what better way to test a candidate's spiritual readiness than to cast him in the role of judge? And since his decision would be subject to ratification by a group of the defendant's peers, what could go wrong?

Everything, McCade thought to himself as a group of Il Ronnians approached the rock. Just about everything could go wrong. Especially considering the fact that he didn't even know *what* crime had been committed. In order to assure their impartiality judges weren't given any information about the crime prior to the trial.

A short Il Ronnian dressed in the uniform of the Star Sept was the first to speak. "I am Sub Sector Commander Deex, and I speak for those who seek redress."

McCade noticed the latticework of scars that crisscrossed Deex's leathery face and the gleam of metal where his left arm should have been.

"Thank you, Commander Deex. Who speaks for the accused?"

Now another Il Ronnian stepped forward, this one attired in the robes of the merchant marine, the nonmilitary ships that conducted commerce between Il Ronnian worlds. "I am Captain Oeem. I speak for the accused."

McCade saw that Oeem was older, his skin hanging in loose folds around his neck and wrists, a slight stoop hinting at years spent within the close confines of merchant ships.

"Thank you, Captain Oeem," McCade replied. He waved his cigar. "Let the accused step forward."

At this point a youngish Il Ronnian took a single step forward. He wore the uniform of a Star Sept Sixteenth Commander, the lowest commissioned rank there was, roughly equivalent to an ensign in the Imperial Navy. He was obviously scared but held his back rigidly erect and ramrod straight. "Sir, I am Sixteenth Commander Reep, sir."

"Thank you, Commander Reep." McCade turned to Deex. "Please read the charges."

Commander Deex stepped forward. "Sixteenth Commander Reep is accused of refusing a direct order from his commanding officer. His offense is made worse by the fact that his group of interceptors were engaged in combat at the time, and by the fact that he is completely unrepentant. His actions set a dangerous precedent and if allowed to go unpunished would endanger all members of the Star Sept.''

McCade stirred uneasily in his seat. There was something funny going on here, at least it seemed like there was, but it was still too early to know for sure. He tapped some ash off the end of his cigar and turned to Oeem.

''Thank you. Captain Oeem? Do you wish to make an opening statement?''

Oeem's tail indicated his assent. ''Yes, I would. I do not contest the fact that Commander Reep disobeyed a direct order from his superior, but maintain that he was correct in doing so, given the situation he found himself in.''

McCade nodded. ''I see. Thank you. Commander Deex, please state the case against Commander Reep.''

Deex stepped forward once again and assumed a position similar to parade rest. If he thought it strange that a human was judging the case, he gave no sign of it.

''Yes, sir. A tenth cycle ago my squadron was assigned to patrol part of the Necta Sector. The Necta Sector forms part of our frontier with the human empire, and because of the unusually large number of star systems in that sector, human pirates use it as a way to enter Il Ronnian space. Over time they have become extremely adept at jumping from one system to the next using planets to shield their activities from our sensors.''

McCade dropped the cigar onto the rock and crushed it out. ''Was your squadron at full strength? And if not, how many ships did you have?''

McCade saw the Il Ronnian's tail twitch in surprise. These were military questions coming from a civilian. And if there was any form of life lower than a human civilian, Deex couldn't think what it was.

Nonetheless this human held a position of power, and power was something Deex understood quite well. He chose his words carefully. The Star Sept was woefully thin along the frontier and in constant need of more funding. On the other hand his superiors wouldn't want him to suggest the frontier was undefended either, especially to a human.

"We had a carrier, two destroyers, and a light cruiser. So while the squadron was slightly under strength, it was more than sufficient for our mission." There. Deex hoped he'd hedged all his bets.

"Thank you," McCade said. "Please continue."

Deex cleared his throat. "Yes, sir. We had been on station for six standard cycles when one of our scouts spotted a formation of five human ships attempting to slip across the frontier. We positioned our vessels along their path and laid in wait. The moment they came into range we issued a warning and called on them to surrender."

This last part wasn't exactly true since it was SOP to fire on human pirates without warning, but Deex couldn't say so, because it wouldn't square with standing orders.

"And then?"

"They tried to run and we opened fire," Deex answered. "The carrier launched a flight of interceptors, and they were engaged by human craft of similar design. It was then that Captain Oeem blundered onto the scene."

"Blundered onto the scene?" Oeem demanded, his eyes glowing under a prominent brow. "How dare you! Since when does a merchant ship on its legal and authorized rounds blunder onto anything? My ship had a perfect right to drop out of hyperspace in that sector. A sector I might add that would be safe for merchant vessels like mine if the Star Sept spent more time on patrol and less time sitting on their rear ends!"

McCade cleared his throat. "Gentlemen, please. You will have your chance in a few minutes, Captain Oeem. Until then Commander Deex has the floor. Go ahead, Commander."

"As I was saying," Deex continued self-righteously, "we had just engaged the enemy when Captain Oeem's ship *arrived* on the scene. As luck would have it, he came out of hyperspace in close proximity to the human ships. Immediately identifying Captain Oeem's ship as Il Ronnian, the humans locked some heavy-duty tractor beams on it and started to retreat while using the merchant vessel as a shield.''

McCade could imagine the pirates' surprise as the Il Ronnian merchant ship dropped out of hyperspace and into their laps. A quick mind had seen the vessel's potential and reached out to capture it. By keeping the merchant vessel between themselves and the Il Ronnian warships the pirates could reduce the volume of incoming fire and escape with their loot. Though careful to conceal it, McCade couldn't help but admire the pirates' audacity.

"And then?"

Deex scowled. "Fearing that we might kill innocent civilians, our commanding officer ordered us to cease fire and withdraw. The pirates would escape but Captain Oeem, his crew, and his passengers would survive."

"And did you follow that order?"

"Yes, sir, all except for Sixteenth Commander Reep." Deex turned to skewer Reep with an accusing look. A look the younger officer managed to ignore by keeping his eyes focused on a spot somewhere over McCade's head.

"And what did Commander Reep do?"

Deex turned back to McCade, and when he spoke his voice was grim. "Ignoring repeated orders to withdraw, Sixteenth Commander Reep dove his interceptor in toward the enemy formation and fired two torpedoes. Both torpedoes found their mark, destroying the largest of the enemy ships and releasing Captain Oeem's vessel. Seeing this, our commanding officer ordered the rest of the squadron to attack and all the enemy ships were destroyed. By disobeying orders Sixteenth Commander Reep endangered civilian lives and those of his comrades as well. Star Sept Command requests that Reep be sentenced to five annual cycles in a military prison and be stripped of his rank."

McCade watched the older officer's words hit Reep one at a time, and knew he'd been had. Although the circumstances were slightly different, the whole thing was too similar to his own court martial to be pure coincidence. Reep and he had both disobeyed a direct order involving civilian lives. And each had been court-martialed as a direct result.

How much information had Swanson-Pierce given them anyway? Enough to give them an edge, to force him into judging himself along with Reep, and to bring it all back. The anger, the fear, and the shame.

McCade forced those thoughts down and back. "Thank you, Commander Deex. Captain Oeem, would you present your side of the case please?"

Oeem's tail twitched in agreement. "I would be happy to. Commander Deex has done an admirable job of explaining how the battle came about, but has chosen to leave out certain facts that have a bearing on Commander Reep's actions. It is well known that the pirates kill Il Ronnian prisoners. There is no market for Il Ronnian slaves within the human empire, and the pirates refuse to feed and clothe us. No, a beam through the head is much quicker and simpler, something that Commander Deex and every other Star Sept officer knows quite well. So when our ships obeyed the order not to fire, they did so for *their* sakes not for *ours*, preferring inaction to the possible criticism that might result from the destruction of my ship."

At this point Oeem held out his right arm to point a quivering talon at Reep. "Only this young warrior had the courage to lay his life and career on the line for us . . . and now, when he should be receiving our highest award for valor . . . he stands before us accused of crimes. Each and every one of us should be ashamed of this day!"

McCade was impressed with Oeem's oratorical skill and decided that in spite of whatever bad luck had befallen Reep up till now, winding up with Oeem as his representative had been fortunate indeed.

"Thank you, Captain Oeem. Sixteenth Commander Reep, is there anything that you'd like to add?"

Reep seemed to grow another inch as he snapped to attention. "Sir, no, sir. Captain Oeem has done an excellent job of stating my case."

McCade nodded. "All right then. I will withdraw to

consider the evidence. When I return I will render my verdict. You may return to your seats.''

As McCade stood and made his way across the rock ledge and into the cave he heard a growing murmur behind him. Twenty thousand Il Ronnians were discussing the case. What would the human decide? A good question, and one he'd like an answer to as well.

It felt strange to enter the great Ilwik's cave. He'd been there countless times in his dreams and knew every nook and cranny of the place. Over there, where a thousand cook fires had blackened the wall, the great Ilwik had prepared his simple meals. And there, where a replica of the teacher's thin mattress lay, was where he'd slept. Slept peacefully until they came in the night to take him away.

And even as they tortured the life from his frail body and milked the tears from his dying eyes, he had forgiven and blessed them saying "I shall return."

And through the bracelet he *had* returned, a thousand times and more, as an unending chain of minds relived his life. And through his teachings the great Ilwik still lived on as an example of what sentient beings could be if they so chose.

A sudden flood of anger and determination rose to fill McCade's mind and emotions. On one level the Vial of Tears was stupid. A religious artifact that the great Ilwik would laugh at if he were alive. Yet on another it had value as a connection between the past and the present, as a symbol of one being's sacrifice, and of the things he'd stood for.

Suddenly McCade was determined to find the Vial of Tears, not just for Sara and Molly, but for the Il Ronnians as well. First however he had to become a full-fledged Ilwik and that meant reaching a judgment about Reep and himself.

Dropping onto the concave surface of a ledge where the Ilwik had loved to meditate, McCade stuck a cigar between his teeth and turned the case over in his mind. Like his own court martial the case revolved around a conflict between military discipline and compassion for others. Like Mc-

Cade, Reep had been forced to choose between the two, and opted for compassion.

Unlike McCade however, Reep had a judge who was both sane and sympathetic. That suggested a verdict of not guilty.

Yet McCade had been an officer himself. He understood the need for discipline and he knew that disobedience had cost far more lives than it had ever saved. What to do?

He rolled the unlit cigar between his fingers, and as he did, an answer came. From his subconscious? From walls that had absorbed the great Ilwik's wisdom? He didn't know or care, but the words certainly came from the great teacher.

"True justice lays outside the jurisdiction of the sept and is not ours to give. All else is symbolic and therefore less than perfect."

McCade stood, stuck the cigar in a pocket, and walked out of the cave with his mind made up.

As he came into sight the murmur of conversation gradually died away until perfect silence filled the room.

Stepping onto the Rock of Truth, McCade looked out at twenty thousand Il Ronnian faces, then down at the three who more than all the rest waited for him to speak.

Deex wore an expression of rock-hard determination, while Oeem looked concerned, and Reep tried to keep his features blank.

McCade cleared his throat, but the cigar butt he'd dropped earlier caught his eye and he bent over to pick it up. He slipped it into a pocket of his cool suit and lifted his eyes to the audience.

Two vid cams moved in for a closer look. "I've reached a verdict that I now submit for your consideration."

Forty thousand red eyes stared back at him in stony silence.

"It is my judgment that both sides of the case have considerable merit. Commander Deex is correct. Discipline is absolutely essential to any military organization, and as Commander Reep admits, he refused a direct order from his commanding officer. In light of that fact a prison sentence and loss of rank seem quite appropriate.''

McCade saw Deex smile and Reep sag momentarily before forcing himself back to attention.

''On the other hand, we must also look at the effect of Commander Reep's actions. Through his valor a loss became a victory, innocent lives were saved, and the pirates were vanquished. Under normal circumstances his name would be submitted for a Medal of Eternal Valor.''

Now Reep brightened and Oeem looked hopeful.

''So as punishment for his crimes I sentence Sixteenth Commander Reep to five annual cycles in prison, suspended, and reduction in rank to noncommissioned officer status. And in recognition of his bravery, I award Commander Reep a Medal of Eternal Valor and congratulate him on behalf of the Il Ronnian people.''

As McCade's words echoed away the silence grew long and thin. And then, just when McCade's heart had begun to sink, a tiny hissing was heard. It grew louder and louder until finally it filled the canyon with its force.

As Deex glowered, Oeem hissed, and Reep grinned, twenty thousand tails lashed their approval. Justice had been served.

Twelve

THE TRANSCAR WAS still moving when the Sand Sept troopers jumped out and checked the platform. After a quick look around they gave the all-clear and McCade stepped out with Teeb at his side.

A long red cape swirled around McCade as he moved, causing bystanders to turn and stare transfixed by the sight of a human Ilwik.

McCade's relationship with Teeb had entered a new phase. The Il Ronnian was genuinely pleased with McCade's success and considered himself to be the human's mentor. In fact, Neem had disappeared, apparently relegated to lesser duties somewhere else.

So Teeb and McCade followed along behind as the Sand Sept troopers cleared a way through the crowd.

"So, Sam, one ordeal ends and another begins."

"True," McCade agreed. "I wish the second ordeal had a better chance of success. Finding the Vial of Tears will be like searching for a grain of sand in the middle of a desert."

Teeb waved the saying away with the tip of his tail. "Do

not be so quick to doubt, egg brother. I once said you would never pass the tests, but now you wear the red, and the people honor you as one of their own. Where one miracle comes another can follow.''

"I hope so," McCade replied doubtfully. "I sure hope so."

And there was reason for concern. McCade had one standard month in which to find the holy relic, and if he didn't, the conservatives would reach consensus and declare war on the human empire. He hoped the human empire was using the time to get ready.

A sharp right carried them into a heavily used corridor. It was full to overflowing with Star Sept troopers, administrative personnel, and spidery maintenance bots. All but the most senior officers hurried to get out of the way, and even they bowed their respect, entranced by the sight of an alien Ilwik.

A host of familiar odors filled McCade's nostrils as they neared the underground hangar. There was the smell of hot metal, the stench of high octane fuel, and the ever-present stink of ozone.

A set of heavy blastproof doors cycled open at their approach and revealed a waiting aircar. It was oval in shape with rows of bench seats. As they took their seats Sand Sept troopers jumped on the running boards and the car began to lift. Seconds later it was scooting full speed toward the far end of the hangar.

The hangar was huge. A deep rumbling came from up above as massive doors slid back to reveal a violet sky. A black wedge slid into sight, its navigation lights strobing on and off as it dropped toward the hangar below. Its shadow quickly shrunk until the rumble of the hangar doors was lost in the scream of the ship's repellors. Dust flared as it touched down and robo tenders rolled out to refuel it.

Farther down five interceptors took off on a training exercise. They seemed to float upward, riding their repellors until clear of the hangar and free to engage their main drives. Then they were gone, mere specks at the far end of long white contrails, arrows headed for the blackness of space.

Meanwhile the aircar passed rank after rank of ships. Some were military, some were civilian, all were in various stages of maintenance or repair. Technicians and robots swarmed around them like acolytes around a series of altars.

And everywhere smaller craft swooped, darted, and dived as they went about their various chores. It made such a spectacle that McCade was taken by surprise when the aircar came in for a landing next to a smallish ship.

Not just any ship, but his ship! McCade ran a critical eye over her hull as he got out of the aircar. *Pegasus* looked just the way he'd left her; in fact, she looked even better. Light reflected off the new coat of heat reflectant paint that covered the hull and a number of small dents had disappeared.

"We took the liberty of doing some maintenance on your ship," Teeb said. "There is no cause for alarm. While we are not really set up for maintenance on human ships, we do capture them from time to time, and our technicians have become quite adept at working on them."

"Well, it certainly *looks* good," McCade said cautiously. "Send the bill to Prince Alexander."

"I would not think of it," Teeb answered with a straight face. "As an Ilwik you have a generous expense account plus a salary of one hundred thousand rang a year."

"Really?" McCade asked, brightening at the thought of additional income. "Well, here's hoping I live long enough to spend it."

Teeb stuck his hand out human style and McCade took it. The Il Ronnian's grip was strong and leathery. "Good luck, Sam."

"Same to you, egg brother," and to McCade's surprise, he found he meant it.

McCade had climbed the rollaway stairs, and was just about to enter the ship's lock when Teeb called after him. "Sam!"

"Yeah?"

"I left some presents for you. I hope you'll find them useful."

McCade waved. "I'm sure I will. Tell Neem I said good-bye." And with that he entered the lock.

It felt good to be inside his own ship again. For one thing it meant he could shed the cool suit and enjoy some honest to goodness air-conditioning.

Stripping to the skin, McCade stepped into the fresher, took a shower, and blew himself dry. Much refreshed, he made for the control room clad in nothing more than a good cigar.

He was humming to himself and emitting small puffs of smoke when he stepped into the control room and came to a sudden stop.

Neem and Reba looked up from their pre-flight check lists and smiled. Reba was the first to speak. "Welcome aboard, Captain. Is that the uniform of the day?"

Thirteen

As PEGASUS HEADED for the human empire McCade relaxed in the ship's small lounge and thought about Teeb's "presents." Reba and Neem. Beauty and the beast.

On many rim worlds Neem would be shot on sight. People don't like Il Ronnians out along the rim, especially on planets like Arno that had been settled by a fundamentalist religious sect. They would see Neem as the devil incarnate and would either shoot him or run screaming for their temples. Either way it was a problem, so Neem would have to stay aboard the ship.

Of course, Neem *could* command the cooperation of any Il Ronnian warships that happened along, and *if* they actually found the vial, he could take it home, a trip McCade could do without.

Even so, McCade wondered if Teeb secretly hoped Neem wouldn't come back at all, and was using the situation to unload a nut case.

Reba on the other hand was a definite asset. Or so it seemed anyway. She was a qualified pilot, a fairly good medic, and fun to look at besides. All skills that could come in handy.

She also swore that her pirate days were over, that she owed McCade a debt of gratitude, and that nothing would give her greater pleasure than to help recover the Vial of Tears. Well, time would tell.

McCade really didn't care as long as she stuck around long enough to give him what he needed most, access to the planet called "The Rock."

McCade requested a Terran whiskey from the autobar and lit a cigar.

Neem entered the lounge, nodded politely, and plopped down in front of the holo player. He put on a set of earphones and stared intently into the holo tank. Another whodunit most likely. The Il Ronnian loved them.

McCade forced his thoughts back to the problem at hand: "The Rock." Once, back during Confederation times, the planet had teemed with life. Thick jungle had wrapped the planet in green, mountains had soared to the sky, and rivers had cut their way down to seas rich with life.

But that was gone now, erased by the hell bombs used to sanitize the planet's surface.

Even then the Il Ronnian empire was expanding, and forts were needed to stop the inexorable advance, forts powerful enough to stand off an invading fleet. So a planet was chosen and prepared. And by the time the engineers finished there was nothing left. Not a tree, not a mountain, not a single body of water. All of it gone right down to the bedrock.

A fortress was constructed. It covered more than a hundred square miles and drew its power from the planet's core. Powerful weapons were placed around the circumference of the planet and aimed toward space. More weapons were placed on orbiting weapons platforms and these too were aimed outward.

Years passed and an Il Ronnian attack never came. The Confederacy destroyed itself instead and gave rise to the

Empire. But some continued to resist the Emperor and in so doing gave the fortress a new purpose.

Thousands of prisoners vanished into the sprawling complex and rechristened the planet "the Rock" after a famous prison on old Earth. And like its namesake the Rock offered no chance of escape. No one could survive on the planet's sterile surface, and even if they did, there was no way off.

Sure, they could take over the complex itself, but why bother? The weapons on the orbiting platforms, like those on the planet's four moons, were now turned inward and manned by marines. Nothing could move without their approval.

As things turned out that was a serious mistake.

The attack seemed like a joke at first. A pathetic attempt by the remains of a rebel fleet to rescue their comrades, strike one last blow for a defeated cause, and go out with a bang.

Though defeated by Admiral Keaton at the Battle of Hell, what was left of the rebel fleet had split up and come back together at prearranged times and places. They knew the war was over, but sympathy for their imprisoned comrades drove them to one last desperate act: An attack on the Rock.

Knowing the planet was heavily defended, the rebels expected to lose, to die fighting, but much to their own surprise they won.

The Imperial Marines fought bravely, but their weapons were aimed in the wrong direction, and they were badly outnumbered. Thousands died.

So the planet's defenses were turned outward once again, and the rebels went about making their prison a home, and in the process transformed themselves as well.

They knew they couldn't rest. The existing supplies of food wouldn't last forever, and given the planet's barren surface, there was no possibility of growing more. Even the thin atmosphere required artificial maintenance.

So the rebels used fighting skills honed during years of war to raid other planets for supplies. They saw themselves as liberators, taking what they needed to continue a glorious cause.

But their victims saw them as pirates, taking what they weren't willing to make themselves, spreading pain and misery wherever they went.

Time passed and once-bright ideals became increasingly tarnished. Loot became the purpose of their existence, and not as a means of mere survival, but as a means of wealth and privilege.

Disliking the term "pirates," they called themselves "the Brotherhood," and styled themselves as an occupational democracy.

But McCade had been to the Rock and seen the way the pirates lived, and there wasn't anything democratic about it. A council made up of a few powerful individuals ran everything and vied with each other for ever larger slices of a rather fat pie.

And they didn't take kindly to unauthorized visitors. McCade knew that from personal experience. On his last visit to the Rock he'd managed to rip them off, blow up half a spaceport, and destroy a number of their ships. As a result he wouldn't be able to sneak in the same way he had before, and once there, he would be in even greater danger.

"A penny for your thoughts."

McCade looked up into Reba's brown eyes. Damn, the woman was pretty. If it weren't for Sara . . . He shoved the thought down and back.

"Only a penny? Surely you're worth more than that. I was thinking of you."

Reba smiled as she dropped into the seat next to Neem. He didn't even look up from the holo tank.

"I'd be complimented if I hadn't seen the holopix of Sara all over the ship. But I have, so I'm worried instead. What's on your mind?"

"I was thinking that you're the key to getting on the Rock. And unless I miss my guess, that's where we need to go."

Reba frowned. "Why?"

McCade examined the ash on his cigar before tapping it into an ashtray. "The vial was taken during a raid, right? And while the pirates who took it didn't realize its true value, I understand the vial is quite pretty, and therefore valuable in its own right. And since all loot goes to the Rock for auction, that's where it went."

"That's true," Reba agreed. "But things sold at auction usually go off-planet with whoever buys them. By now the vial could be anywhere."

McCade nodded his agreement. "Exactly. But once we find out *who* bought the vial, we can track them down. Make sense?"

Reba's eyes dipped toward the deck and back up again. She had reservations but wasn't willing to share them.

"It makes sense," she agreed reluctantly. "But how will I get you onto the Rock? And more importantly, how will you get off? I was on patrol when you trashed port twelve. But I heard about it, and I know the executive council would love to get their hands on you. They might allow you to get dirtside, but they'll never let you go."

McCade blew smoke toward the overhead and smiled. "Then we won't tell 'em I'm there."

Fourteen

SPIN WAS A desolate place, so unremarkable that its name stemmed from its one redeeming virtue, earth normal gravity. Gravity that served to hold a small collection of dilapidated domes in place in spite of the fact that it wasn't worthwhile.

The planet had little to recommend it. The vast majority of its surface was dedicated to rocky wasteland, and if Spin hadn't marked the nexus of two minor trade routes, it would've stayed uninhabited.

McCade had been there once before. A fugitive called Crazy Mary had led him there after a long and weary chase. He'd ordered her to surrender, but she'd just laughed and gone for her blaster as she had so many times before.

But this time it was her turn to fall, it was her body they dumped outside for the scavengers to pick clean, and it was someone else who walked away.

McCade felt his cheek twitch as Reba lowered *Pegasus* onto the scarred surface of Spin's single spaceport.

Three other ships had landed there before them. There was a beat-up Confederation-era freighter, a sturdy-looking tug, and a sleek little DE that had "pirate" written all over it.

Good, McCade thought to himself. The first part of the plan had fallen into place. With a little luck the rest would follow. He eyed the DE's scarred flanks.

Destroyer Escorts were just right for small one-ship raids. They were fast, heavily armed, and large enough to carry some loot. Small stuff like isotopes and rare gems.

The com screen swirled to life as Reba cut power to the ship's repellors. On it was a man who just barely qualified for the name.

Hair crawled over his bullet-shaped head, sprouted from his ears, and covered his face. His eyes blinked constantly as he spoke.

"It's gonna cost you a thousand credits to park that play pretty on my pad."

Reba scowled. "A thousand credits my ass. A hundred, and not a penny more."

The man grinned evily. "Your ass ain't worth a thousand credits. Not even here. Nine hundred."

Reba made a rude gesture. "Two hundred."

The man displayed yellow teeth as he laughed. "Seven hundred."

"Three hundred."

"Six hundred."

"Four hundred."

"All right, all right. Five hundred credits. But don't expect any free drinks."

The screen went suddenly black.

"You humans crack me up," Neem said from the hatch. As usual he wore a red heat cape wrapped around his skinny torso. "All that bargaining for a simple landing fee. Whatever for?"

"Entertainment mostly," McCade replied as he released his harness. "The less formal entertainment there is, the more bargaining we do. Now, does everyone understand the plan?"

Reba nodded and Neem's tail twitched in agreement.

"Good, let's get ready."

An hour later Neem stood by the lock to see them off. "Good luck, Sam, I hope everything goes smoothly."

"Same to you, Neem. And remember, keep a close eye on the sensors. If someone tries to board, dust 'em off."

"Dust 'em off," Neem said experimentally. "I like that. Another alternative to waste 'em, grease 'em, and ice 'em. You humans certainly have a grisly language."

"You've been watching too many holo dramas," McCade said patiently. "Just do it, okay?"

"Okay," Neem replied happily. "If anyone tries to board, I'll dust 'em off."

"Good. I'll see you in a week or so."

Pulling the rebreather down over his head, McCade checked the neck seals and looked at Reba. Hers was already in place and she gave him a thumbs-up.

McCade palmed the lock control and waited while the inner hatch cycled open. When Reba stepped through he followed.

Both waved at Neem until the hatch had cycled closed. There was a wait while Spin's noxious atmosphere was pumped in, and a slight pop as the hatch cycled open and pressures were equalized.

Needless to say there were no robo stairs to meet them, so Reba was forced to deploy a ladder and wait while McCade clanked his way down it. The leg shackles were noisy and slowed him down.

As Alice's one and only peace officer, McCade had other more modern restraints aboard the ship. But the leg shackles were the most dramatic by far and therefore appropriate to the situation.

As Reba made her way down the ladder McCade took a look around. The DE looked larger now, looming above him like some sort of metal monster, partially hidden by wisps of poisonous fog. Was that gun turret pointed his way on purpose? Or had it been positioned like that all along?

His thoughts were interrupted as Reba gave him a shove

and growled, "Get a move on, stupid. This ain't no sight-seeing trip."

McCade tried to catch himself, but his leg shackles tripped him and he fell.

Reba jerked him to his feet with a growl of frustration and gave him another shove.

Head hung low, shackles clanking, McCade shuffled toward the nearest dome. Someone could be watching or monitoring their radio traffic, so Reba was right to establish their relationship.

But did she have to shove so hard? Should he put this much trust in her? What if she betrayed him the moment they got inside?

Then Neem would come to his rescue. He'd try anyway. While Reba was asleep the two of them had cooked up a plan. Neem would lift *Pegasus* on her repellors, cripple the DE, and cut a hole through the skin of the main dome.

Assuming Neem managed to carry out the first part of the plan, McCade would don his rebreather, release his leg shackles using the electronic key taped to the inside of his left forearm, and escape via the newly created exit.

The plan was complicated and vulnerable to all sorts of unforeseen problems, so McCade hoped they wouldn't be forced to use it.

Reba gave him another shove and he stumbled forward.

Piles of debris were heaped left and right. It was SOP to throw garbage outside the lock until it threatened to engulf the dome itself. At that point someone would climb aboard an ancient crawler and shove the garbage into a nearby ravine.

Reba palmed the lock. The hatch made a grinding sound as it cycled open. It too was overused and undermaintained.

Long before it was fully open the hatch began to iris closed. They hurried to get inside and just barely made it. Seconds later a noisy pump went to work evacuating Spin's noxious atmosphere.

A slush of water and mud covered the bottom of the lock. Plastic sacks full of garbage lined both sides of the chamber and the walls were covered with a variety of graffiti. None was especially original.

The place was still the same. Fortunately he wasn't. In the unlikely event that someone remembered him, McCade figured that his five-day growth of beard, filthy rags, and beaten demeanor should be a sufficient disguise.

A tired buzzer announced a breathable atmosphere and the green indicator light in McCade's rebreather confirmed it. As he shuffled toward the inner hatch McCade pulled the rebreather down off his face and let it hang by its straps.

Continually urged on by a series of shoves and insults, McCade followed a muddy path down a poorly lit corridor and into a circular room.

The air was thick with blue smoke. It hung in layers of blue-gray with the heaviest smoke on the bottom and the lightest on top.

A few things *had* changed since he and Bloody Mary had faced each other in the center of the room. The bar was kitty corner from where it had been, a new holo tank took up a large part of one wall, and the layer of grease that covered everything was even thicker.

Conversation stopped and every head turned as they entered. Not too surprising since they were the most exciting thing to happen all day.

McCade was careful to maintain his submissive posture as Reba pushed him toward the center of the room and swaggered along behind. Watching from the corners of his eyes he saw the bar was about half full. It wasn't difficult to sort them into groups.

The pirates sat by themselves toward one corner. There were eight of them, nine if you counted the woman passed out on the floor. Their table was loaded with empties. They seemed dazed as if the two strangers were apparitions only half seen and partially understood.

Unless they were short on personnel McCade figured there were two or three additional crew members still aboard the DE.

The male pirates watched Reba with a certain amount of

interest, but no one jumped to their feet and called her name, so none of them knew her. Good. They had a story prepared just in case, but McCade didn't want to use it.

The freighter's crew sat on the far side of the room. They were as far away from the pirates as they could get and still be in the same bar. McCade didn't blame them. It's a wise sheep who stays as far away from the wolves as possible.

There were four of them. The captain was a solid-looking black woman in her forties. To her right sat a youngish-looking woman with the flashes of a power engineer on her nonreg cap. Next to her sat a brutish-looking Cellite and a beat-up android. The latter was sucking an electronic cock-tail via a wall outlet. Like the pirates they'd left one or two people aboard their ship.

There was a scattering of other people in the room as well, an older man and a boy who might have been a match with the tug, plus the usual assortment of drifters.

One of these was a man of indeterminate age with flat dead eyes, expensive clothes, and a blaster with custom grips. Just as the pirates looked like what *they* were, the gambler looked like what *he* was. His eyes drifted across McCade and came to rest on Reba. A smile touched his lips.

"Greetings. At the risk of sounding trite, what brings someone like you to a place like this?"

Reba smiled. "Gravity, the need for a number four power board, and a powerful thirst."

The gambler nodded understandingly. "Would you care to join me? I don't bite."

Reba looked around as if considering her other options.

It's perfect, McCade said to herself, don't overact.

McCade heaved an internal sigh of relief as she grabbed a chair and shoved him toward another. "Sure, as long as you don't mind gark breath here. He gets into trouble if I leave him aboard ship alone. Isn't that right, gark breath?"

Reba kicked McCade just as he tried to sit down. He fell and the pirates laughed.

McCade swore under his breath as he picked himself up and claimed a chair.

"What was that, gark breath?"

"Nothing," McCade mumbled.

"Good," Reba said, turning toward the gambler. "Now where were we?"

"Just getting acquainted," the gambler replied smoothly. "Can I buy you a drink?"

"Does a Zerk monkey like fava fruit? You bet your ass you can."

The gambler summoned one of the saloon's two staff members, a slovenly woman who doubled as Spin's only prostitute, and ordered drinks. After accepting two glasses of black brew, the gambler paid and offered Reba a toast.

"To quick money and just enough time to spend it."

"Amen."

Both upended their glasses. Reba choked, coughed, and came up grinning. "I don't know what that was, but I'll bet you could run my ship on it."

"They call it a Tail Spin," the gambler answered as a deck of cards appeared in his hands.

Reba eyed the cards and licked her lips. A nice touch, McCade thought admiringly. Not only was Reba keeping her word, she was doing it with a certain amount of class.

The gambler saw her hungry look and smiled. The cards jumped from one hand to the other and back again. "Do you play?"

"Sometimes," Reba answered with just the right amount of hesitation. "Not very well though. Would you be interested in a friendly game of Flash?"

The cards made a graceful arc as they rippled through the air to patter down in front of her. The gambler smiled. "Deal."

Fifteen

REBA WAS GOOD. Maybe *too* good since she was winning instead of losing.

It was the gambler's deal. He'd just lost a long series of small pots, and although he kept his face professionally blank, McCade could see the sheen of perspiration that glossed his forehead. The gambler had upped the ante in hopes of recouping his losses. But would it work? If not, he'd lose his entire stake. A stake he'd need to buy his way off Spin. It was just a theory, but a theory that fit the situation like a glove, and would explain the gambler's anxiety. An extended stay on Spin would be less than pleasant.

The cards made a gentle slapping sound as they hit the surface of the table. Before long there were ten cards face-down in front of each player. Reba looked up. "Dealer flashes first."

The gambler inclined his head slightly. Long white fingers lifted the cards one at a time and showed or "flashed" them at Reba. She had approximately one second to see and memorize each card before the gambler flipped it over and tucked it into his hand.

Then it was Reba's turn. She held each card up for a full three or four seconds before hiding it away. But the gambler was *still* losing in spite of that advantage. Maybe Reba had a better memory than he did, or maybe she just out classed him, but whatever the reason things were *not* going according to plan.

McCade shifted his weight from one side to the other. He wanted to yell, "Lose damn it, lose!" but bit his lip instead.

Now both players were taking turns replacing up to five of their ten cards in an effort to build a full system. A full system included twin stars, six planets, a comet, and one moon. But a full system was pretty rare, so lesser hands usually won.

So when Reba said, "Read 'em and weep, a full system takes the pot," McCade groaned in disgust.

The gambler managed to smile as Reba raked in the pot, but McCade could see the perspiration running down his neck. Chances were the gambler was close to tapped out. If so, he'd pull out pretty soon.

And the gambler was just about to say something when the pirate saved the day.

The pirate was young, no more than twenty-five, and walked across the room with a drunken swagger. He wore a slug gun low on his right hip, like someone who fancies himself a quick-draw artist and worries about what other people think.

From McCade's point of view the pirate was a godsend, just what he'd hoped for in the first place and failed to get.

"Any chance of dealing myself in?"

The gambler spoke quickly. "It's all right with me if the lady has no objection." Maybe another player would change his luck and reduce the magnitude of his losses.

Reba made a show of thinking the proposition over as she tossed off her latest Tail Spin.

Finally, when McCade thought she'd pushed it too far and the pirate would leave in disgust, she gestured toward an empty chair. "Sure, why not. Let's see the color of your money."

The pirate fumbled around in a pocket for a moment before dragging out a wad big enough to choke an Envo Beast. He slapped it down on the table, called for a drink, and shuffled the cards.

Reba's luck took a turn for the worse a few minutes later. The pirate won, and continued to win, until the gambler's eyes narrowed in suspicion. Was she throwing the game? But that wouldn't make any sense. Why cheat to lose? Besides, he was winning, and so long as that continued he'd keep his mouth shut.

An hour passed, and as it did Reba became increasingly careless, forgetting which cards her opponents had and making a series of stupid mistakes.

The others put it down to her heavy drinking, and McCade would have too, except he'd seen her surreptitiously pour them into the semiliquid slush that covered the floor.

Finally it was over and Reba's money was nearly gone. A large pot occupied the center of the greasy table and Reba burped as she threw down her remaining credits. "Well, thaz it, gentlemen. Outside of gark breath over there, and juz enough to cover a number four power board, I'm broke."

The pirate looked down at his hand and up to Reba. His bloodshot eyes gleamed with anticipation. "Fine. Throw in gark breath and I'll show you what I've got."

A frown creased Reba's forehead as though she was trying to understand the pirate's proposal and, finding that hard to do, was pretending to think it over.

The gambler had decided something was fishy. He didn't know what and didn't care. He was slightly ahead and wanted to stay that way. He spread the fingers on both hands. "It's getting too rich for me. I fold."

Reba tried to focus bleary eyes on his face. She nodded heavily. "Zur, just when things get interestin' you bail out. Well, not me. I hereby add gark breath to the pot. Read 'em and weep."

Though not overly thrilled about the name "gark breath," McCade was happy that things were finally moving in the right direction. He watched Reba and the pirate spread their cards out on the table.

There was a long silence.

Reba was the first to frown, followed by the pirate, followed by McCade himself. He couldn't see the cards from where he sat, but something was wrong.

While Reba *should* be frowning, the pirate *should* be jubilant, and he wasn't. Suddenly McCade understood. Reba had won! The miserable so and so had won the pot! All that work, all that hobbling around in shackles, all of it a waste of time!

And that's when Reba did the only thing she could. She swayed in her chair, held a dramatic hand up to her forehead, and fell over backward. Her chair hit the floor with a tremendous crash.

Conversation stopped, heads turned, but things were back to normal a few seconds later. No big deal, just another drunk hitting the floor. A somewhat routine occurrence in that or any other rim world bar.

The gambler looked at the pirate. The pirate looked at the gambler. They grinned. "Fifty-fifty?" the gambler asked.

"Done," the pirate agreed. And the two men wasted little time splitting the pot. With that accomplished they turned to McCade.

"You have a ship and I don't," the gambler said thoughtfully. "Give me a hundred credits and gark breath is yours."

McCade knew that fifty percent of a prime slave was worth more than a hundred credits and so did the pirate. "Agreed. One hundred credits it is."

The pirate counted out a hundred credits, stepped over Reba's prostrate body, and jerked McCade to his feet. McCade cringed, thanked the pirate for hitting him, and shuffled toward the lock.

Meanwhile the rest of the pirates were headed for the lock as well. Two were busy trying to out belch each other, while the rest bumped into furniture and cracked crude jokes.

McCade felt his new owner give him a push, and heard him say, "Hurry up, gark breath, we're headed home."

McCade did his best to snivel. "And where would that be, master?"

"Why the Rock, gark breath, the Rock. Where else would members of the Brotherhood go?"

Sixteen

McCade spent the first part of the trip locked up in a small storage compartment with a broken-down maintenance bot. McCade ignored the robot at first, but eventually the loneliness wore him down, and he tried to make conversation.

"Hi there. What's a nice robot like you doing in a place like this?"

There was a whir of servos as the robot turned its bulbous head. "I have a defective logic board. I am awaiting repair."

McCade nodded sympathetically. "That's a tough break. Say, you're a maintenance bot, aren't you?"

"That is correct."

"Well, if you're a maintenance bot, and you need maintenance, why not fix yourself?"

Time passed during which the robot made no reply. Finally, just as McCade was about to drift off to sleep, the robot spoke.

"I apologize for my delayed response. At first I couldn't understand why you would ask me such a question. Then I realized that you were stored in here for the same reason

I was. When did your logic board burn out?''

McCade smiled in spite of himself. ''I think it was the moment when I allowed Swanson-Pierce to rescue me from Molaria.''

''Oh,'' the robot replied, and lapsed into silence.

Time passed and eventually, after much boot-licking, McCade was allowed to perform menial chores under the watchful eye of his owner.

His owner was an up and coming young pirate who went by the name of Ace, but was actually named Harold, and who lived in fear that his friends might discover his terrible secret.

But it wasn't Ace's friends who discovered the secret, it was McCade. There he was, cleaning up the pirate's filthy cabin, when he came across a stash of letters. They all started out with ''Dear Harold,'' and were signed, ''Love, Mommy.''

Thus armed McCade blackmailed his owner into some extra food and the occasional cigar. When you're a slave the small comforts mean a lot.

Meanwhile, Ace took very little interest in McCade's past, accepting his lies with bored indifference, eager to sell him and drink up the profits.

This attitude suited McCade to a T, so he made himself the model slave, always cooperative and eager to please.

This strategy worked so well that after a while the crew began to take him for granted and allowed him a certain amount of freedom.

As a result he was in the control room as the ship approached the first weapons platform. The weapons platforms were located approximately one light out from the Rock and constituted its first line of defense. They were heavily armed, completely automated, and capable of identifying friendly ships via a code printed into each vessel's atomic structure. If you had the code, you could pass; if not, boom!

McCade knew that much from past experience. What he

didn't know, and wanted to find out, was whether the pirates had added anything new since then.

So McCade was swabbing the deck when the DE came into range of the nearest weapons platform. Never mind the fact that robots normally swabbed the deck. The pirates never asked any questions as long as he did something menial.

"Platform alpha sixteen coming up, Skipper." The pilot sounded bored. And why not? The DE had the proper codes and he knew it.

"That's a roger," the skipper replied, looking up from a skin mag. "Hey, gark breath, how 'bout a cup of coffee?"

"Right away, sir," McCade sniveled, and shuffled his way toward the small alcove at the rear of the bridge.

The pilot ran his hand through a shaggy head of brown hair, picked his cavernous nose, and tapped out a short rhythm on his keyboard.

Peeking out from the small pantry, McCade saw the words "Brotherhood vessel 6456 Delta cleared for planetfall" appear on the pilot's com screen and vanish again as the pilot cleared his board.

"We're cleared for planetfall, Skipper."

"That's real good, Murph. Hey, gark breath! Where the hell's my coffee?"

McCade had an idiotic grin on his face as he shuffled his way over and spilled scalding hot coffee on the captain's leg.

"You idiot!" The skipper jumped to his feet, hit the coffee pot with his arm, and sloshed more hot liquid onto his right foot.

There was quite a commotion for a while as the captain swore and hopped around the control room on his one good foot with McCade in sniveling pursuit.

Finally the officer stopped in one place long enough for McCade to dab ineffectually at his leg and analyze what he'd seen.

The system hadn't changed, and later on that would play

an important part in his escape, assuming there *was* an escape. First of course he'd have to get on the Rock, avoid detection, and find the vial. Just take it one step at a time, he told himself, that way you won't realize how completely stupid the whole thing really is.

The skipper was still glowering a few hours later when the pilot put the ship down on the planet's light side on the inner ring of Port Seven.

Being devoted to both military and commercial enterprises the Rock had some sixty spaceports, number seven being entirely dedicated to the repair and maintenance of raiders.

McCade had never seen someone clean out their ears and land a spaceship at the same time before, but the pilot not only pulled it off, he did it rather neatly as well. The landing jacks made only the slightest bump as they touched down.

A small army of robo tenders scuttled out to refuel and perform maintenance on the ship as the whine of the ship's repellors died away.

Eager to see their families, or to tie one on, the crew wasted no time gathering their personal belongings together and heading for the main hatch. And, as one of Ace's belongings, McCade found himself wearing shackles and struggling to keep up with his owner.

As he clanked his way down the robo stairs to the durocrete pad below, McCade took a look around. This was a military spaceport, but with the exception of the ships themselves, it looked a lot like the commercial version he'd seen during his previous visit. Long orderly rows of ships, and beyond them the endless vista of black rock that stretched to the far horizon.

And interspersed among the ships were the black towers. Each one was a hundred feet high and topped off with a bulbous turret that bristled with weapons and sensors. Up there, behind armored glass, members of the Brotherhood's planetary police stood watch, and the knowledge sent a chill down McCade's spine.

Wouldn't they just love to catch him! On his last visit he'd almost leveled a spaceport, destroyed dozens of ships, and caused the destruction of an orbital weapons platform. Now he was back, and if the police found out, slavery would look good by comparison.

His heart leaped into his throat. There were four members of the planetary police waiting at the edge of the pad! Their black uniforms and military appearance were supposed to strike fear into the hearts of miscreants everywhere and it worked. The muscle in McCade's cheek started to twitch and his emotions clamored for attention.

"Run for it!" they screamed. "Kill! Run! Hide! Do something!"

"Now wait a minute," his mind replied. "This doesn't make sense. They couldn't know about me. They're here for some other reason."

"Oh, yeah?" his emotions asked. "And what the hell do you know? We'd have been dead years ago if we listened to you. Hide! Run! Kill!"

McCade was looking for a place to hide when the line jerked to a halt and the pilot dumped his flight bag in front of the police. It was mostly dirty laundry and as the police pawed through it they made a number of crude jokes about his purple underwear. Of course! A customs check!

"See," McCade told his emotions, "there was nothing to worry about."

"Maybe," they grudgingly admitted, "but let's delay the celebration until *after* the customs check."

Having finished with his flight bag, the police were running sensors over the pilot's body. It made sense. Without a search the crew would start to skim loot off the top of their haul and the Brotherhood would lose out.

The pilot was cleared and the line jerked ahead. As Ace stepped up to the table he gestured for McCade to follow.

The police flicked a retinal scanner across Ace's eyes while they pressed his right hand onto an electro pad. Somewhere a computer compared the incoming prints with the ones on file, achieved a match, and signaled its approval.

Three of the police had their visors down, all the more to intimidate you with, but the fourth wore hers tilted up. And surprise, surprise, she had a sense of humor.

"Name?"

"Ace Javers."

The woman consulted her hand-held comp. "Gee, Ace, looks like we've got a mix-up here. The computer thinks you're some guy named Harold."

Ace mumbled something.

The policewoman pretended not to hear. "What was that? Harold? Well, why didn't you say so in the first place? Glad we settled that. Now, who's the guy in chains? Prince Alexander?"

"We call him gark breath," Ace responded, eager to regain some of his lost composure. "I won him playing Flash."

"Witnesses?"

"The skipper was there."

"Good enough. We'll take him from here. Usual deal, ninety percent for you, ten for the Brotherhood."

"Sounds good."

"Okay, give me your seal."

Ace pressed his right hand on the electro pad for a second time and was waved through the checkpoint. He took off without so much as a backward glance at McCade.

The policewoman gestured for McCade to step forward. "Okay, gark breath, let's check you in."

McCade was scanned, printed, and cleared all within a couple of minutes. Even so the seconds dragged by like hours, each one bringing the very real possibility that the central computer would cough up his real identity and finish his mission right there.

But his real identity had never been properly recorded during his previous visit to the Rock, so nothing happened.

The policewoman looked up from her comp and smiled. "Hey, buddy, you're now WM 89546. It ain't much, but it sure beats the hell out of gark breath. Next!"

Two hours and a series of rides later McCade found himself in an all-male holding pen. For someone who'd done time in Molaria's Pit 47, it was all too familiar: the hopeless eyes of his fellow prisoners, the subjugation of the weak by the strong, and the desperate scramble for food. McCade faded into the dog-eat-dog structure of it without conscious thought.

But all things considered, the holding pen was nicer than Pit 47. It was well lit, fairly spacious, and furnished with durasteel furniture. You couldn't move it, you couldn't burn it, but you could sit on it and McCade did.

There were other differences as well. Where Pit 47 had housed the same men for months at a time, there was constant turnover in the holding pen, and that slowed the emergence of a strong pecking order. And that was fine with McCade because beating the hell out of people was not his idea of a good time.

"Aha," said a voice from behind him. "A fellow anomaly I trust?"

McCade turned to find himself face-to-face with a little man with bright inquisitive eyes, a long, thin noise, and ears that stuck out like handles on a cup. Like McCade he was dressed in little more than rags.

"An anomaly?" McCade asked.

"Why yes," the man replied. "You know, a deviation from the norm."

McCade smiled patiently. "Yes, I know the meaning of the word, I just don't understand how it applies."

The little man looked surprised. "You don't? How strange. It's quite obvious to me." The bright little eyes looked McCade up and down. "You're in good shape, you're well fed, and you're wearing nice rags."

"Nice rags?"

"Um-hmm," the little man said. "Nice leathers that were ripped and torn to look like rags. And there's your body language. While most of us are scared, wondering what'll happen next, you're relaxed. So, you're an anomaly. And where there's an anomaly there's a reason.''

"And you have a big mouth," McCade said thoughtfully. "Which doesn't qualify you as an anomaly, but could get you in deep trouble."

The little man looked around to make sure that no one else was listening. "Don't worry. Your secret's safe with me." He stuck out his hand. "They call me Chips."

As McCade shook the other man's hand he found it was dry and surprisingly hard. "Chips?"

"Yeah, Chips, like in computers. That's what makes me different than the rest of this herd. I'm smarter than they are."

McCade nodded thoughtfully. "That's just great, Chips, except for one little thing. If you're so smart, how come you're a slave?"

Chips dismissed McCade's comment with a wave of one hand. "This is a temporary inconvenience, nothing more. "I work—or should I say 'worked'?—for a large conglomerate. Maybe you've heard of it. Mega Mining and Metals. No? Well, it's *big*, take my word for it, and I am, or *was*, their top programmer.

"I was on my way to restore a major systems failure on some godforsaken asteroid when the company speedster came out of hyperspace right on top of a pirate raider. We tried to run, but they put a tractor beam on us and reeled us in like a dead carp. So, here I am, but," Chips added brightly, "not for long."

Chips looked around and lowered his voice into a conspiratorial whisper. "How would you like to get off this rock?"

McCade had run into his share of deluded prisoners before, Pit 47 had housed some real lulus, but he decided to play along. Although Chips seemed like a flake, he'd seen through McCade's disguise with disconcerting ease and that suggested hidden depths.

"I'd love to get off this rock," McCade replied, "assuming I can pick the time."

Chip's smile revealed some expensive dental work.

"Good, because all I need to get us off-planet are these"—
he waggled his fingers—"and a willing endomorph." Chips
looked McCade up and down like a chef selecting a side of
beef.

McCade sighed. From gark breath to endomorph in a
single day. Sometimes you just can't win.

Seventeen

As SLAVE MARKETS go it wasn't too bad. It was fairly clean for one thing and they didn't beat you for another. Not much anyway. This didn't stem from latent humanism but from a reluctance to damage the merchandise. And being part of the merchandise, McCade approved.

At the moment he and Chips were standing in a line that led out and onto a small stage. An underground transcar ride had brought them here from the central holding pens.

Like everyone else they were naked, stripped of even their rags, and exposed to the world. McCade was reminded of his journey through the corridors of Molaria, and decided to handle it the same way, forcing himself to stand tall and look people in the eye.

Everything was painted an eye-searing white. White walls, white ceiling, and a white floor.

It seemed strange at first, until McCade realized that the white background made them easier to see. Especially for eyes used to a level of illumination higher than earth normal, and presumably there were some such in the audience.

But no amount of white paint could cover up the feel of the place, the stink of their sweat, or the fear that oozed out through their pores to fill the air. It was a bad place, a place where sentients were bought and sold like hunks of meat, a place from which all compassion had long since fled.

Beyond the stage there was row after row of theater-style seating. The seats were already half full and the would-be slave buyers were still flooding in. A more variegated lot McCade had never seen.

There were plenty of humans, the usual scattering of Zords, and even a Lakorian or two. Not too surprising since all three races were regular participants in the slave trade.

There were some exotic species scattered throughout the hall as well, but it was hard to tell what they looked like due to their bulky atmosphere suits.

What McCade wanted to see but didn't was Reba. She was supposed to land, buy McCade, then set him free. A workable plan given the fact that she was a pirate in good standing. But the seats were filling up now and Reba was nowhere in sight.

It was as if Chips could read his mind. "So where's your friend?"

McCade frowned. "How the hell would I know? I imagine she'll show up any minute now."

Chips shook his head sadly. His voice was sorrowful, as though McCade had somehow led him astray. "Face it, Sam, she ran out on you. She wasted your friend, took your ship, and sold it. I should never have listened to you. Now it's too late to use my plan."

McCade had provided Chips with a somewhat sanitized version of his current situation. While he'd mentioned two friends, he'd left out the fact that Neem was alien, and Reba a somewhat secretive pirate.

Instead, he'd left the impression that he was trying to

recover something the pirates had stolen from him, and that Chips could help. In return McCade had promised to get Chips safely off-planet.

By agreeing to McCade's plan, Chips had given up one of his own. Which was just as well since it called for an endomorph like McCade to incapacitate several guards while Chips accessed the Brotherhood's computer system.

Chips swore that once he obtained access to the Brotherhood's computer system he could fiddle the records and set them free. The only problem was that he hadn't figured out how to get them off-planet afterward.

McCade thought the little man's plan was less than perfect, and would probably generate more than a few unexplained corpses, possibly including his own.

But he did see a certain value in having his own computer expert, assuming of course that he managed to escape from his present situation. What better way to get a lead on the Vial of Tears than to take an unauthorized peek at the Brotherhood's records?

But everything hinged on Reba setting him free so he could set Chips free. Why had she deserted him? Maybe she was scared, or maybe she'd lied to him from the start, but it would be easy for her to kill an unsuspecting Neem and go her merry way. And there wasn't a damn thing McCade could do about it either. Especially if he was busy harvesting yirl deep in the jungles of some godforsaken jungle planet.

His thoughts were interrupted by the auctioneer's deep baritone. "If you'll finish taking your seats, the auction will begin in a few moments."

There was a rustling as latecomers found seats, the hum of servos as their chairs adjusted to a variety of physiological differences, and the low murmur of conversation as the buyers gossiped among themselves.

McCade knew that others would follow the action as well, watching the auction on closed-circuit holo and bidding via computer terminal. The thought cheered him.

Maybe that was the answer. Maybe Reba would bid by computer.

He remembered what it was like. The vast dome filled with thousands of sentients, the tower that dominated its center, and the countless terminals used to buy and sell stolen merchandise. Merchandise so cheap that victims sometimes chose to buy their goods back from the pirates rather than replace them from other sources.

Yes, Reba could be in that dome somewhere preparing to buy his freedom, but deep down he knew it wasn't true. If she came, she'd come here and do it directly.

McCade scanned the audience one last time, hoping, praying that he'd spot Reba's pretty face among them. No such luck. All he saw were hard faces and calculating eyes.

"Greetings on behalf of the Brotherhood," the auctioneer said portentously.

He was a tall, slender man with slicked-back hair and a pencil-thin mustache. He enjoyed being the center of attention and performed his duties with a theatrical flourish.

"We have some prime humanoids for you today," he said cheerfully, "and I'm sure you'll find something to meet your particular needs. And now time's money so let's get started."

A couple of bored-looking police types shoved a man forward. He was middle-aged, somewhat overweight, and on the verge of tears.

"An excellent specimen," the auctioneer said approvingly. "A little exercise will turn WM 7896-A into a prime field hand."

The auctioneer glanced at a hand-held comp. "Skills include operation of simple machinery, some ability at advanced math, and—you'll love this—he plays the violin! Is anyone out there assembling a symphony orchestra? If so, this is the one for you!"

There was general laughter from the humans in the audience and a variety of other noises from the aliens as well.

Bidding started rather low and, in spite of the auctioneer's best attempts to drive it upward, ended with a high bid of three hundred and forty-six credits.

The middle-aged man looked even more dejected as he was herded to one side where a female Zord used her single eye to inspect her newest possession.

He was the first of many. Some made a fuss, crying or calling out for help, but most were outwardly calm, hiding their thoughts and feelings behind blank faces. Then as their new owners led them away, the line would jerk forward and the police would shove someone else toward the middle of the stage.

Finally it was McCade's turn and he scanned the audience one last time. Maybe Reba had slipped in unobserved, maybe he'd missed her the first time around, maybe everything was all right. But no such luck. Reba was nowhere to be seen and his time was up.

The police shoved him forward and the auctioneer tapped his shoulder with a silver pointer. "Now here's a decent-looking field hand. He's in good shape as you can see, young enough to survive in a hostile environment, and healthy as a horse. He has no special skills to speak of, but how much skill does it take to lift a shovel?"

The audience laughed appreciatively and the auctioneer gave a small bow. "Do I hear an opening bid?"

A tough-looking man in black leathers made the first bid. "Three hundred."

"Three fifty." The second voice emanated from a creature in a four-armed atmosphere suit. McCade tried to remember a race with four arms but couldn't.

"Four hundred," said the man in leather. He looked annoyed.

"Four hundred and fifty." The voice had a hollow metallic quality as it came over the suit's external speakers.

McCade felt a heavy object drop into the pit of his stomach and hoped the man in leather would win. There was something ominous about the four-armed creature. Its suit was black and kind of bulky through the middle as if it had a midsection similar to a spider's, and worst of all was the fact that you couldn't see its head. Where a human's eyes would be there was a band of polarized plastic that circled all the way around the thing's helmet. Did it have eyes in the back of its head? There was no way to tell.

McCade was not given to xenophobia but the thing made his hair stand on end. Looking around he saw that others felt the same way too. No one wanted to look directly at the thing, as if afraid of what they might see. Even the auctioneer looked over rather than directly at it.

That was bad enough. What was worse was the thing's motives. It didn't breathe oxygen so what would it want with a human slave? A number of possibilities popped into McCade's mind and none of them were very pleasant.

"Five hundred." The man was beginning to sound bored, and based on the bidding that had gone before, McCade knew they were reaching the upper limits of his worth.

"Six hundred," the creature said levelly, "and five hundred apiece for the next three in line."

Chips snapped to attention, viewing the creature with alarm. "What the hell . . ."

"I'll pass," the man in leather said, "they're all yours." He took his seat with an expression of disgust.

McCade looked on with alarm as the auctioneer nodded his understanding and said, "Going once, going twice, gone. Congratulations, my friend, you've got a fine group of humanoids there. Pay the cashier and collect your merchandise. *Bon appétit.*"

There was nervous laughter as the creature lumbered over to the cashier's window, paid for its slaves, and watched the police shackle them to a length of durasteel chain.

Chips was behind McCade with the two newcomers behind him. One was a big black man and the other was white. Both did their best to avoid looking at the four-armed alien.

Once the four humans were secure the alien used one of its four arms to gesture toward the door. "Move."

"Thanks a lot," Chips whispered as they stumbled forward. "I'm not only a slave, I'm a slave to some alien geek. God knows what it will do with us."

"I hope it gets you to shut up," McCade growled.

Obviously offended Chips pursed his lips and pretended McCade wasn't there.

Once they were outside the slave market they followed the alien into a steady stream of traffic. Slaves were a common sight on the Rock and attracted little attention, but four-armed aliens were something else; even the police hurried to get out of the way.

They hadn't gone far when the alien turned in at one of the planet's less reputable hotels. There was a low rumble of conversation between the alien and the hotel keeper followed by the flash of credits changing hands.

Then they were herded into a small room. The alien pointed at McCade. "You. Come with me. The rest of you wait here. Food will come soon."

McCade's stomach growled at the thought. Why couldn't he stay? But a nerve lash had appeared in one of the alien's gloved hands and it left him little choice.

The thing unshackled the others, ushered McCade into the hall, and locked the room behind him. The fact that this was possible suggested that the room had served a similar function before.

"Come." So saying, the alien lumbered down the hall as if sure that McCade would follow.

McCade thought about running, but knew he wouldn't get far wearing shackles, and decided to obey. Maybe later on he'd find a way to overpower the alien and gain the upper hand.

The alien stopped in front of another door. It swung open at its touch. "In there."

McCade entered rather cautiously since he was unsure of what he might find inside. He needn't have bothered. This room was a shabby duplicate of the first one. He heard the door close behind him and turned just in time to see an incredible sight.

The alien was using two arms to unscrew its helmet. What

the hell was going on? Was the alien planning to commit suicide right there in front of him?

The helmet squeaked as it turned and McCade backed away waiting for some kind of noxious atmosphere to spill out.

It didn't. Instead the arms lifted the helmet up and away to reveal Neem's smiling countenance. "Don't just stand there, Sam, find some blankets. It's colder than the tip of an asteroid miner's tail in here."

Eighteen

THE COMPUTER CONSOLE was first class just like everything else in their suite. Chips cracked his knuckles experimentally as he sat down in front of it. He wore a big grin as he brought the first screen up and entered the system. To him this was an electronic jungle in which he was the skilled explorer avoiding all manner of dangers and steadily closing in on the hidden treasure.

McCade checked the door to make sure it was locked and sat down across from Neem. The power lounger sighed softly as it adjusted to his body and radiated a gentle warmth. McCade plucked a cigar from a nearby humidor and puffed it into life. When he spoke it was through a cloud of smoke. "How much does this suite cost per rotation anyway?"

Neem shrugged as he turned up the heat on his power lounger. "As you humans would say, it beats me. Since I don't plan to pay, I never asked."

Nonpayment of bills. One more offense added to our growing list of crimes, McCade thought to himself. Well, why not? What's another crime more or less when you've already broken every law short of murder?

"So," McCade said, waving his cigar to include the entire room. "Perhaps you'd be kind enough to explain how we came to be here?"

The tip of Neem's tail had slipped up and out of his coat collar. It signaled his agreement. "As things turned out, your departure from Spin triggered an unfortunate series of events. As you'll recall, I was supposed to monitor the ship's sensors in case of trouble. So there I was, monitoring my life away as you were taken aboard the pirate ship. 'So far so good,' I said to myself as your vessel lifted, 'Sam is on his way.'

"Reba came out of the dome shortly thereafter and I opened the main lock to let her in." The Il Ronnian shook his head sadly. "It was a mistake to trust her, Sam. You should have left her on Imantha."

"Oh, really?" McCade inquired dryly. "Wasn't it Teeb who sent her along? And you too for that matter?"

"Let's not quibble over details," Neem replied loftily. "The point is that your treacherous female pulled a blaster on me and forced me off the ship."

McCade raised an eyebrow. "You're in surprisingly good shape for a corpse."

"The female did allow me a breathing unit," Neem conceded, "but that was her only kindness. The moment I was clear of the ship she lifted."

McCade felt a moment of grief. He'd grown attached to the little ship and hated to lose her. Still, a ship is a ship, and not very important when compared to the big picture. Or so he told himself. It didn't seem to help much.

"So what then?"

"So there I was," Neem said dramatically, "cast adrift on the uncharted sea of an alien culture, unable to enter what little shelter there was, and vulnerable to whatever predators might happen along."

"Please," McCade responded, "spare me the sob story. You found a way off Spin or you wouldn't be here."

"Yes," Neem agreed shamelessly, "utilizing my tremendous resourcefulness I found a way to escape the terrible predicament you left me in. Do you remember the small tug?''

McCade thought back to their landing on Spin. He remembered the DE, a freighter, and, yes, a small tug. "Yeah?"

"I stole it," Neem said proudly. "I waited in the shadows near the tug's lock for the crew to approach. Time passed, and with each second that ticked by, my precious supply of oxygen became smaller and smaller.''

McCade groaned. "Please, spare me the melodrama.''

Neem ignored the interruption. "Then, just when my breathing device was almost empty of life-giving oxygen I saw them. Two humans approaching the tug. Even though I was gasping my last breath I waited for the first one to palm the lock before I hit the second one over the head. It took two blows because the first one hit the forward edge of his breathing device and bounced off.

"Having heard the disturbance, the first human turned and came to the second one's assistance. Such was my speed and skill that I was able to disable him as well, dragging both clear of the tug's repellors prior to entering the ship and taking off.''

McCade had conflicting emotions. Having your ship stolen out from under you was about the worst thing that could happen short of death itself, and to have it happen on a planet as desolate as Spin, well that made the situation even worse.

On the other hand he couldn't help but admire Neem's resourcefulness, especially since the Il Ronnian was the human equivalent of a college professor. "I'm amazed, Neem . . . it was a nice piece of work."

"Thanks, Sam, I'm kind of proud of it myself. I'm not much of a pilot as you know, but the tug was equipped with automatics, and having had some experience with *Pegasus*, I had little difficulty getting into space.''

"And then?"

Neem's tail assumed a posture of doubt. "Then I didn't know *what* to do. I checked the tug's computer and found coordinates for the Rock, but based on what you'd told me, I knew I wouldn't get past the weapons platforms.

"I'm ashamed to say that I was just about to run home with my tail between my legs, a rather strange saying for you humans to have by the way, when I stumbled across the answer.

"As I entered the new course into the tug's computer it asked me if I *really* wanted to enter a new set of coordinates or use the last ones instead. Just out of curiosity I asked what the last ones were. Well, I couldn't believe my eyes when the coordinates flashed on the screen."

"Your next destination was the Rock," McCade guessed.

"Don't be silly," Neem replied tartly. "I was lucky, but not *that* lucky. No, the next destination was the Asod Cluster." Neem paused dramatically. "To tow a disabled ore barge to guess where?"

"The Rock," McCade said, exhaling a long, thin stream of smoke.

Neem's tail drooped. "You guessed."

"Sorry," McCade said unsympathetically. "So you went to the Asod Cluster. Then what?"

"It was fairly simple after that," the Il Ronnian admitted somewhat reluctantly. "Thanks to the ship's automatics I was able to assist two other tugs in pulling the barge out of orbit. We locked all four vessels together via tractor beams and made a synchronized hyperspace jump."

McCade winced at the thought. It was a common practice but it was damned dangerous. One miscalculation, one hyperdrive slightly out of phase with the others, and all four ships would be lost. Blown up? Forever adrift in hyperspace? No one knew for sure, and McCade had no desire to find out.

"So," Neem added matter-of-factly, "once we cleared hyperspace it was simple. The pirates were expecting us so we sailed right past the weapons platforms. Then we placed the barge in orbit, landed for refueling, and went our separate ways.

"By then I was determined to take Reba's place and

obtain your freedom. A disguise seemed in order and it was a simple matter to cut up three of the tug's spacesuits and construct a somewhat exotic-looking alien. I thought the extra arms were especially effective, didn't you?''

"A nice touch," McCade agreed dryly as he stubbed out his cigar. "I owe you one, Neem. A big one."

"Yes, slave, you certainly do," Neem replied through a big grin. "And the next time I purchase slaves, remind me to go for quality rather than quantity."

"How *did* you pay for us anyway?" McCade asked. "And why buy four instead of one?"

Neem gave a good imitation of a human shrug. "I had some time to kill during the hyperspace shift from the Asod Cluster to the Rock. I used it to crack the tug's safe. When I got the safe open I found a thick wad of credits inside. It was as simple as that.

"Once on the Rock I donned my disguise, took a taxi to the hotel where my other two slaves are still under lock and key, and waited for the auction. One rotation later it started, and not wanting to seem too interested in any one human, I bought four. The rest is, as you humans would say, history."

"Paydirt!" The voice belonged to Chips. "They've got one helluva good system, I'll give them that, but not good enough to foil old Chips! I went around their blocks, defeated their traps, and fooled their tracers. In a few moments you'll have a print-out of all the loot taken from Il Ronnian space within one standard week of the date you gave me. Complete with description, estimated value, and final disposition. Then all we gotta do is grab the vial and haul ass."

"That's great!" McCade said, jumping to his feet. "Chips, you're a genius."

The small charge went off with a loud cracking sound and the triple locked door flew open. A small army of armored police rushed in and took up positions around the room.

They didn't say anything. They didn't have to. Their

drawn weapons said it all. McCade, Chips, and Neem all froze without being told.

Smoke billowed, eddied, and was sucked toward the nearest vent. That's when Reba stepped into the room and smiled. "Hello, Sam. Greetings, Neem. I couldn't help but overhear that last comment via the bug in the ventilator. Chips is many things . . . but a genius isn't one of them."

McCade treated Chips to a withering look.

The little man spread his hands apologetically and said, "Ooops."

Nineteen

"SAM MCCADE, I'D like you to meet Sister Urillo. Sister Urillo, this is Sam McCade."

Sister Urillo was a cyborg, a beautiful cyborg, but a cyborg nonetheless. It hadn't always been so. During a raid on Carson's World a surface-to-air missile had ignored the electronic countermeasures built into her aerospace fighter and hit one of her stubby wings. Her ship crashed a few seconds later.

Her copilot pulled her from the burning wreck, but she had massive injuries, and even with an unusually fast air evac, she just barely survived.

Doctor after doctor said she'd be lucky to live out her life in a nutrient tank, little more than sentient tissue, stored away in some dark corner of a hospital.

But Urillo refused to give up. She said "yes" to the countless operations, she said "yes" to the experimental bionics, and she said "yes" to the pain.

And finally, when all the parts of her body were meshed into a unified whole, she went a step further. She made a decision to love and accept her new body. So while others might have hidden their bionic parts, Sister Urillo flaunted hers, treating them as ornaments and using them to her advantage.

She had rich brown eyes and a beautiful face. It was almost untouched by the crash, the single exception being her left temple and cheek where smooth brown flesh gave way to golden metal. The metal had been sculpted to match the other side of her face. Fanciful patterns had been engraved into the metal, moving and flowing to surround and enhance the single ruby set into her cheek. It glowed with internal fire and flickered with each movement she made.

Her shoulders were of gleaming chrome giving way to golden arms and fingers. Her red dress was cut low to reveal most of her remaining breast and all of its metal twin. The metal breast was perfectly shaped and tipped with a ruby nipple.

Lower down her dress fell into sculptured lines around beautiful legs, one brown and one chrome. They took turns appearing and disappearing through slits designed for that purpose.

And Sister Urillo's appearance didn't end there. Her combination office-living quarters were a carefully designed extension of her body. A high-tech, glass-topped desk served to complement and echo her metal parts while the rest of the furniture was soft and brown like her remaining flesh.

McCade noticed that her voice had a lilting quality and was only slightly distorted by a hidden speech synthesizer. "Greetings, Sam McCade. Although we haven't met, I was present the last time you left the Rock. It was an expensive and rather spectacular sight."

Even though her hand was metal covered by a thin layer of golden plastiflesh, McCade found it warm to the touch. Some sort of heating element woven into the plastic?

He smiled wryly. "My apologies, Sister Urillo. Had I known that such a beautiful woman was present I would have stopped to introduce myself."

"It's better that you didn't," Urillo replied with a laugh. "I would've been forced to blow your head off."

She turned to Reba. "He's annoying but gallant as well. You didn't tell me that."

Reba looked from Sister Urillo to McCade and shrugged. "Sam is full of surprises. Like his transformation from slave to computer thief for example. It was a mistake to under-estimate him."

"I'm glad you admit it," Sister Urillo said as she went behind her desk. "A little humility is a useful thing. Both of you, please, take a seat. McCade . . . you may light one of those god-awful cigars if you wish . . . though Reba may object."

"Go ahead," Reba said as she selected a seat. "My cancer shots are up-to-date."

The invitation bothered him. He wasn't sure why. Maybe it was their complete control of the situation, or maybe they'd taken the fun out of it, but whatever the reason he refused.

"Thank you, ladies," McCade said, dropping into the deep comfort of an over-stuffed armchair, "but I think I'll pass."

"All right then," Sister Urillo said, her eyes suddenly hard. "Let's get down to brass tacks. By now you realize Reba's something more than a damsel in distress. Most of the time, when she isn't allowing herself to get captured during Il Ronnian raids, she's one of my security agents. I sit on the Brotherhood's governing council and have responsibility for planetary security. So when Reba left Spin, she came straight to me."

McCade nodded. Well, it was his own fault. He'd been suspicious, just not suspicious enough. "I suppose Chips works for you as well?"

Urillo nodded approvingly. "Yes, Chips works for us on a part-time basis."

"Then why the charade?" McCade asked. "Why not grab me off the top?"

Reba shrugged. "We wanted to see if you would contact any Imperial agents. There are some but we don't know who they are."

"And," Sister Urillo added wryly, "you did contact an agent. A crazy Il Ronnian who found a way to escape from Spin, bypassed our security systems, and bought you on the open market. We actually lost track of you for a while, and if it hadn't been for Chips, you might have escaped."

Reba nodded soberly. "Another mistake on my part. I should've killed Neem, but I couldn't bring myself to do it."

"That *was* a mistake," Sister Urillo agreed, "but in retrospect it was a good mistake."

"Speaking of which how *is* Neem?" McCade asked. He hadn't seen the Il Ronnian since the police had broken in.

"Your friend is fine," Urillo replied calmly, "which brings us to you." She leaned forward in her chair. Her eyes narrowed and the light sparkled off the ruby in her cheek. "I should kill you and use your body to help rebuild our damaged soil. And if it weren't for this absurd religious relic, that's exactly what I'd do. But Reba tells me the Il Ronn are ready to come after this thing, and if they do, the Rock's the first place they'll stop. And while we might stand 'em off for a while, there wouldn't be much left when they got done, and some stupid vial isn't worth dying over. So this is your lucky day, McCade. Instead of winding up dead, you're going to find the relic and give it back to them."

McCade felt a big emptiness in the pit of his stomach. "Find it? You've already got it. The Vial of Tears was taken during a raid on an Il Ronnian planet and brought here."

Sister Urillo leaned back in her chair and steepled her golden fingers. Light winked off her forearms and danced across the ceiling. "Unfortunately that's not the case. Oh, it was taken during a raid all right, but it wasn't brought here, and we aren't sure where it is."

"You see," Reba added, "the raid was unsanctioned."

"Meaning that while the raid was carried out in our name and using our ships, we didn't authorize it," Urillo added. "That particular raid was led by Mustapha Pong, an ex-colleague of mine and a complete rogue."

"I was looking for leads to Pong's whereabouts when I was captured," Reba explained. "We want him just as much as the Il Ronn do."

"Exactly," Sister Urillo agreed, chrome flashing as she crossed her long legs. "So I want the two of you to stop screwing around and go find him."

Twenty

TIN TOWN. THOUGH not a town in the normal sense of the word the name fit. First because Tin Town was made of metal, and second because it qualified as a collection of inhabited dwellings, and that's what a town is.

So what if this particular town was in orbit around a planet, was equipped with hyperdrive, and had once been an ore barge? To the ten thousand five hundred and sixty-five sentients who lived there, Tin Town was home.

As *Pegasus* drew closer McCade dimmed the main viewscreen. Tin Town shimmered with light. Much of it came from the signs that covered its hull. They rippled, flashed, and pulsated, advertising everything from ***HOT SEX***, to Clyde's Cyborg Clinic. "Check in and check us out."

Some of the light came from Tin Town herself. As the hull turned on its axis an endless array of solar collectors flashed in the sun and generated a belt of light. In addition, there were the winking navigation beacons, the glow of welding torches, and the occasional blue-white flare of steering jets when ships jockeyed for position.

McCade had never been to Tin Town before, but like

everyone else, he'd heard of it. The habitat had been founded some seventy years before by a group of people who disliked government of any kind. They believed everyone should accept responsibility for every aspect of their lives, and having done so, they owed nothing to others. As a result they were commonly referred to as "Loners."

The group first tried to live out their philosophy on a succession of rim worlds. Things would be fine for a while, but after a while new settlers would come along and conflict would soon follow.

The new settlers would want to establish a fire department, or a police force, or some other public service, and they'd propose a government to organize and provide it.

The Loners would object, suggesting a privately owned enterprise instead. They felt each person should be free to support the service in question or go without.

"But what about the destitute?" the settlers would ask. "Don't we have a moral duty to help them?"

"Not at all," the Loners would reply. "With the exception of a very few who should borrow money and start again, the destitute failed to provide for themselves. Now they want *us* to take responsibility for *their* lives and protect them from the consequences of their own folly. That's not fair. Why should we support a government we don't want or need?"

Needless to say the rest of the settlers went right ahead and formed governments without them, provided services, and imposed taxes. At this point the Loners were forced to pay or leave, and time after time they left, eventually settling on some other planet where they were forced to start all over again.

Eventually some of the Loners grew tired of the unending struggle and decided on another course of action. If they couldn't have their own planet, they'd create an alternative. A habitat large enough to hold them but small enough to control. Their habitat would be mobile too, so they could leave unfriendly environs whenever they wished, including human space if that became necessary.

Research showed that a conventional ship wouldn't be big enough and a custom-designed habitat would be way too expensive. The solution strangely enough was an ore barge. Unlike most ore barges, this one was equipped with drives of its own and was fairly new to boot. The barge had come onto the market when the company that owned it went out of business. Due to its unusual size and design, other companies had declined the opportunity to buy it.

But the barge was perfect for what the Loners had in mind so they formed a corporation and bought themselves a dream. True to their philosophy each person bought as much of the barge as they could afford, paid for those services they wished to receive, and were in all other respects free to do as they wished.

To protect their newfound freedom the Loners instituted a policy of strict neutrality toward all governments, planetary and galactic alike, and in doing so made themselves accidentally rich.

Throughout the history of human civilization there's been a need for neutral ground. A place where enemies can meet, where money can be stored, and secrets can be kept.

Given their fanatical desire for independence, their utter pragmatism, and their ability to run from trouble, the Loners were perfect candidates to fill this need. And fill it they did, opening banks, storage vaults, and a broad range of related services.

Due to their prosperity, others were eager to join them. And pragmatists though they were, the Loners didn't care whether the newcomers understood or approved of the underlying philosophy, only that they lived in accordance with it.

Time passed, and before long there were more people than space to put them in, so additions were approved. There was no reason to limit mass since Tin Town was too large to negotiate a planetary atmosphere, and doing so would have compromised its security.

As a result the barge began to change shape. Her once-smooth hull grew bumps and bulges as sections were enlarged. Two globular liners were connected to the barge's bow and stern, making her the bar between two huge dumb-bells. Then a forest of sensors, weapons platforms, and cooling fins appeared along with the now-famous name "Tin Town."

A soft chime interrupted McCade's thoughts as the com screen lit up. Where he expected to see a face, there was a request for a damage deposit instead. A rather *large* damage deposit.

Although the Loners placed no political restrictions on their visitors, they did insist on insuring themselves against financial loss. After all, a town without laws tends to attract some nasty visitors and without some sort of controls would soon cease to exist. Therefore each visitor was required to produce a rather substantial damage deposit before they were allowed to land.

The Loners were willing to accept a variety of assets including cash, ships, family members, specialized equipment, bodily organs, and anything else of recognized value.

McCade typed *Pegasus*'s name and legal description onto the com screen, palm printed the agreement, and swore as it faded from sight. If he or any member of his crew caused damage to Tin Town, or any of its permanent residents, *Pegasus* would be forfeit.

He didn't like it, but according to Sister Urillo, there wasn't much choice. Her sources said that Mustapha Pong had been sighted three times in recent months, all of them in Tin Town, and all of them in the company of a local businessman named Morris Sappo. The habitat was in orbit around a planet called Lexor at the moment, but there was no way to tell if that was a significant part of the Sappo-Pong relationship, or just happenstance. But it could be important, and since no one knew when the Loners might decide to move Tin Town somewhere else, time was short. If McCade wished to find Pong or, failing that, Sappo, he'd have to visit Tin Town, damage deposit and all.

Threading his way through a maze of orbiting ships and

free-floating junk, McCade guided *Pegasus* into the lighted maw of Tin Town's main hatch.

The hangar was huge, taking up all of what had once been the barge's number three hold. All sorts of ships formed orderly rows to the right and the left. There were scarred freighters, sleek little one-man scouts, richly appointed space yachts, sturdylooking tugs, and a scattering of pirate raiders. The latter were not too surprising since Tin Town was one of the few places pirates could openly visit.

Lowering *Pegasus* into her allotted berth, McCade killed the repellors and turned to his companions. "Welcome to Tin Town, a monument to money, and an eyesore in the sky. All ashore who's goin' ashore."

Though Neem and Reba didn't seem excited by the prospect, they disappeared into their cabins and showed up a few minutes later ready to go.

Reba was dressed in faded coveralls. She wore a blaster in a cross-draw holster and had a throwing knife sticking out of her right boot top.

McCade had debated the merits of taking Neem versus leaving him on the ship and, based on the Il Ronnian's previous success, had decided to take him along.

Neem was a vision in black. Black helmet, black visor, and a long black cloak that concealed his tail. He had blasters concealed in his copious sleeves, a wicked looking sword strapped across his back, and variety of knives scattered about his person.

McCade wasn't sure how Neem would react to actual combat, but he certainly *looked* like death incarnate, and maybe that would help.

A shuttle bus arrived a few minutes later, sealed its lock against the ship's and welcomed them aboard. There was something wrong with the vehicle's voice simulator that caused it to drop every fourth word.

"Welcome to Tin . . . We hope you . . . enjoy your stay . . . You may pay . . . cash or we . . . be glad to . . . you a line . . . credit secured by . . . damage deposit. Please .,. . the payment plate . . . you wish to . . . credit.''

McCade palmed the plate and gave thanks that Swanson-Pierce had provided a thick wad of expense money. If a shuttle ride cost fifty credits a piece, how much would a hotel room be?

The shuttle stopped twice to pick up other passengers before heading for the main terminal. Except for a birdlike Finthian and a wealthy-looking Cellite, it was a largely humanoid crowd.

The Cellite wore richly detailed pajamas. They swished softly with each movement of his stocky body and gave off a spicy scent. He wore a matching skullcap on his rounded head and, lacking a nose, breathed through his thin-lipped mouth.

As he boarded the shuttle the Cellite's eyestalks darted this way and that, examining his fellow passengers with the friendly curiosity of a small child. Then the alien caught sight of Neem and developed a sudden interest in a viewport.

McCade grinned. Neem's new disguise was having the desired effect.

The shuttle made lock-to-lock contact with the main terminal, disgorged its passengers, and issued a broken invitation for others to come aboard. Most were more drunk than sober and barely able to stagger aboard with the help of handholds and crewmates.

Reba grinned. ''This place makes Spin look like a nursery school.'' She had to yell it over the noise of the crowd.

McCade nodded and motioned toward a broad corridor that led away from the lock and toward glittering lights. ''Make a hole, Neem. We'll be right behind you.''

''Having a couple of humans behind me is not my idea of a dream come true,'' Neem replied good-naturedly, ''but everyone should live dangerously once in a while. Follow me.''

And they did. Both sides of the corridor were lined with wall-to-wall shops: restaurants, bars, whorehouses, cloth-

ing stores, equipment dealers, banks, medical clinics, and
weapons dealers.

And these were not passive enterprises but centers of
frantic activity packed with merchandise and staffed by sentients ready and eager to unload their present stock and bring
in more.

Signs blinked, hawkers yelled, and robots scurried
through the crowd bleating out their prerecorded messages.
"Dark dreams! Dark dreams! A place where dark dreams
come true! Corridor five, cross tunnel fourteen. Dark
dreams! Dark dreams!"

The air was filled with a heady mix of smells. Smoke,
perfume, food, sweat, and other odors too faint to identify
all fought for dominance.

McCade noticed that the crowd seemed to bunch up
around the more popular haunts and thin out again to pass
others by. And although the crowd was made up of all sorts
of sentients, all had one thing in common. It was a look, a
look that said they needed to acquire something, or satisfy
some hidden need before time and money ran out, and they
were forced to leave.

And here and there along the edges of the crowd the
predators waited, their restless eyes skimming the crowd in
search of profit or pleasure. There were all sorts: whores,
pimps, thieves, pirates, mercenaries, bounty hunters, and
more, all waiting, all living off the weakness of others.

But the tall black thing didn't look weak, and neither did
the man and woman who strode along behind it, so the
predators watched but made no move. Strength is difficult
to gain and easy to lose so eventually the black thing might
still be theirs.

"The House of Yarl." That was the name Sister Urillo
had provided and it was right where she'd said it would be,
just off the main corridor along cross tunnel twenty-three.

The name was deeply etched into a brass plate that graced
an otherwise nondescript metal door. It hissed open at
McCade's touch. As the bounty hunter stepped inside he
found himself in a small but richly appointed lobby.

A middle-aged woman with a kindly face and two wings of dark hair looked up from a comp screen. "Welcome to the House of Yarl. My name is Portia. How may I help you?"

"We're friends of Sister Urillo's," McCade replied. "She recommended that we stay here."

"How nice," the woman replied evenly. "How *is* Sister Urillo these days?"

"The kinesthetic feedback unit you sent her is much better than the old one. She can dance now."

When Portia smiled her entire face lit up. "Excellent! It is as I hoped. There was a time when she loved dancing as much as flying. One, two, or three rooms?"

"Three," Reba said firmly.

"I don't know about you, but I feel insulted," McCade said to Neem.

"Maybe it's those cigars," Neem replied. "They're enough to drop an Ikk at thirty yards."

The woman tapped away at her keyboard and looked up at the comp screen. "Your rooms are ready. Palm the counter, then palm the doors."

McCade pressed his palm down on the counter, followed by Reba, then Neem.

Portia frowned at the alien's gloved hand but decided to let it go. Anyone wearing gloves could open the thing's door, but whatever lurked behind that visor could take care of itself and wouldn't need any advice from her.

They were just turning to go when Portia turned on her professional smile. "Thank you for choosing the House of Yarl and have a nice stay."

McCade smiled, nodded in her direction, and decided that he'd be satisfied if he got off the habitat alive.

Twenty-one

THEY'D BEEN WALKING for about twenty minutes and the bright lights were far behind them. Every third or fourth light was burned out or shot out, McCade couldn't tell which.

The walls were covered with graffiti and garbage lined both sides of the corridor. The air was humid and carried the strong scent of urine. Every society has an underside and this was Tin Town's.

The people who passed them were the dregs of a society focused on self. They padded the length of Tin Town's less traveled corridors like human vultures, hoping to find the leavings of some predator, or to encounter a victim so weak that they could make the kill themselves.

But the threesome were well armed and moved with the confidence of those who know where they're going and why. And since the vultures were ever fearful of becoming victims themselves, they gave the strangers a wide berth and went in search of weaker prey.

Nonetheless, there was the very real possibility of an

ambush. The corridor practically screamed, "Danger! Run for your lives!"

So while Reba managed to *look* calm, her right hand hovered over her blaster, and there was a tightness in the way she moved. Her eyes jerked toward McCade when he spoke and then darted away.

"Where did you say we were going again?"

Reba frowned. "We're looking for a good restaurant. Pay attention, Sam. We're looking for a man called Scavenger Jack. Sister Urillo has him on a retainer. If Pong's here, Jack will know."

McCade was about to say something along the lines of "Well, excuse me," when Neem snarled at the both of them.

"Cut the chatter, you two. Unless you'd like to come up and trade places with me."

Il Ronnians are partially nocturnal and have better night sight than humans so Neem was leading the way. But he didn't relish the assignment and wanted them to know it. Each side tunnel was a potential threat, and if someone started a firefight, he'd be the first to die.

"Tunnel eighty-seven. We're getting close," Reba said, pausing to read faded numbers. "Scavenger Jack lives in ninety-one right."

They passed three more tunnels without incident and found themselves in front of one marked "91." Unlike most this one was partially lit.

McCade stepped into the tunnel. "Watch our backs, Neem. We'd be like rats in a trap if this tunnel dead ends."

"Rats in a trap," Neem said experimentally. "I like that. Is it similar to being up feces creek without a paddle? And why travel on a creek filled with feces anyway?"

"Not now, Neem," Reba replied impatiently. "Just watch our backs." And so saying she followed McCade into the tunnel.

Neem started to make a rude gesture with his tail but remembered that she couldn't see it and wouldn't understand even if she could. He settled for a rude noise instead.

Turning, he backed his way up the tunnel, watching the main corridor for signs of trouble.

They were about a hundred feet into the tunnel when they heard the scream. It was long, drawn out, and undeniably human.

McCade drew his blaster and broke into a run. Another scream followed the first, this one going even higher, before dying into a low gurgle and disappearing altogether.

Up ahead a door slammed open and a shaft of light hit the far side of the tunnel. A shadow hit the wall as a man stepped out and turned their way. He took one look and drew his slug gun. "Come on, guys! We've got company!"

The man used a high velocity slug to punctuate his sentence. The slug blew air into McCade's ear as it passed, hit the overhead, and screamed down the corridor. The chances were slim that it would go through the habitat's hull, but it could happen. Stupid asshole.

McCade squeezed his trigger and punched an energy beam through the man's chest. As he fell over backward more men came through the door and leaped his body. They had better sense and opened up with energy weapons.

Now Neem and Reba had joined the fray. Bolts of blue energy screamed up and down the tunnel. The two groups came together with a collective grunt just as another man fell. Knives flashed in the dim light and it was each person for himself.

McCade found himself paired off with a man in a blue uniform. He was short, ugly, and smelled of cheap cologne.

McCade tried to use his blaster but found his wrist locked in a grip of steel. Light flashed off the other man's blade and McCade blocked it with a grip of his own. Now the two men tried to best each other through strength alone.

Though a full head shorter than McCade, the other man was as strong as an ox, and it was soon apparent that he'd win. He held his knife edge up, and in spite of McCade's best efforts, each second brought the shining steel closer and closer. Any moment now and McCade would feel the first pinprick as the knife point broke his skin. Next would come the excruciating agony as the cold steel slid into his guts. His belly jerked back at the thought.

Neem's voice came from behind. "Turn him around!"

McCade found that if he pulled with one arm and pushed with the other he could turn his opponent to the right.

"Get ready to die," the man rasped through yellowing teeth. "I'm going to split you open like a ripe fava fruit."

McCade didn't waste precious energy on a reply. Instead, he used all of his remaining strength to push and pull at the same time.

It was then that he heard the whicker of cold steel and Neem's Il Ronnian war cry. As the alien swung into sight his sword was already in motion and McCade did his best to duck.

The razor-sharp steel made a sucking sound as it passed through the man's neck and came out the other side. There was a gout of bright red blood as the man's head went one way and his body went another. They hit the metal deck with a double thump.

McCade swayed slightly as he looked around. His arms still hurt where the other man had gripped them. A glance informed him that Reba was okay and that the rest of the assailants had fled. Neem was using a corpse to wipe the blood off his blade.

Seeing McCade's look, Neem grinned behind his visor. "While in college I took a course in the fabrication and use of ancient weapons. Standard stuff for anthropologists and, as it turns out, quite useful as well."

McCade shook his head in amazement. "You never cease to amaze me, Neem. You *are* a crazy bastard."

"You can say that again," Reba agreed. "And a good thing too. Come on. Let's see what's inside."

McCade went through the door fast and low, his blaster searching for a target. There was none.

The inside came as a complete surprise. He'd expected some sort of hovel, a metal cave complete with piles of junk, and a grizzled old man who called himself "Scavenger Jack."

Nothing could've been further from the truth. Far from being a metal cave, Scavenger Jack's foyer was larger than McCade's hotel room and better decorated as well. The floors were marble, the walls were covered with rich red fabric, and the light fixtures dripped crystal. For some reason the man chose to live in a remote and almost deserted part of the habitat.

"Over here." Neem had pushed a door open with the point of his sword.

McCade followed the Il Ronnian through the door and found himself in a formal sitting room. It was filled to overflowing with richly upholstered furniture, fine paintings, and small pieces of Finthian sculpture. Something caught his eye and he moved over to investigate.

"This is amazing," Reba said quietly. "Who'd believe you could find something like this just off tunnel ninety-one? Scavenger Jack sure knows how to live."

"And how to die," McCade added. "Look at this."

Scavenger Jack was lying behind a couch. In life he'd been a handsome man with curly brown hair and a thick mustache. He wore a surprised expression as if he'd known how things were supposed to turn out and this wasn't it.

McCade couldn't blame him. Scavenger Jack was not a pretty sight. Neither was the knife that protruded from his chest. First they'd worked him over, which explained the screams and the condition of his fingernails. They'd pried them off one at a time. McCade wondered why. Did it have something to do with Pong? Or was it totally unconnected? There was no way to tell.

"Damn." Reba made it a comment and an expression of sorrow all in one.

"Yeah," McCade agreed. "Not a very nice way to go."

"There's no such thing as a 'nice way to go,' Neem observed. "And I suggest we leave lest we suffer a similar fate. They might come back."

Neem's suggestion made a lot of sense so they wasted

little time slipping out the door and into the tunnel.

There was no way to tell if Scavenger Jack had a next of kin, or if the habitat's founders believed in concepts like legal inheritance, but they closed the door just in case.

It closed with the solid thump common to bank vaults everywhere, and now that McCade looked more closely, he realized the door and frame were made of hull metal. Though a bit eccentric, Scavenger Jack was no fool.

All of which made McCade curious. Given the fact that an energy cannon wouldn't even scratch the door, how had the killers managed to get inside?

The obvious answer was that Scavenger Jack knew his killers and decided to let them in. That, plus his surprised expression, suggested friends. Or people he *thought* were friends.

The bodies were right where they'd left them and Reba's knife flashed as she cut something off the headless corpse, stuck it in a pocket, and moved down tunnel.

The walk back was long but uneventful. As they approached the hotel McCade saw a number of police and, what with his bloodstained clothing and heavily armed companions, felt more than a little conspicuous.

But this was Tin Town, and unless the police had some reason to suspect that someone had attacked one of *their* clients, then there was nothing to fear.

McCade decided to visit his room prior to joining the others. So when he entered Neem's room a half hour later he was showered, shaved, and feeling much better.

McCade noticed that the Il Ronnian had the room temp up to max and was about to complain when he remembered the sound that Neem's sword had made as it passed through the short man's neck. The heat suddenly seemed like a minor inconvenience and he said "hello" instead.

Besides turning the room into an oven, Neem had taken the opportunity to shed his disguise. Freed from all constraints his tail danced this way and that as he spoke.

"Welcome, Sam. Reba has come up with some rather interesting information."

"Good," McCade said as he dropped into a chair. "We could use some interesting information right about now."

Reba had her boots up on a coffee table and was using a piece of the hotel's promotional material to fan herself. She looked unhappy. "Well, it's interesting . . . but not very helpful. You remember the short guy Neem made even shorter?"

McCade nodded grimly. "Who could forget?"

"Well, I cut the insignia off his uniform on the way out. I showed it to Portia and she says it belongs to Morris Sappo's household troops."

McCade lit a cigar and used the time to think. Pong had been seen with Sappo on each of his recent trips to Tin Town. They knew that from the reports Scavenger Jack had filed with Sister Urillo. So it seemed that Pong and Sappo were financially linked and maybe even friends. It wasn't difficult to imagine ways in which one of Tin Town's foremost businessmen could assist a renegade pirate and turn a profit in the process. Having broken off his relationship with the Brotherhood, Pong would have to sell his loot somewhere, and Tin Town was the perfect choice.

Given that, and given the fact that McCade was on Pong's trail, it seemed likely that Sappo's troops had murdered Scavenger Jack in an effort to protect Pong's privacy. But how had they known?

"It appears that there's a leak in Sister Urillo's organization," McCade said, expelling the words along with a column of smoke. "Someone informed Pong and/or Sappo that we were on the way."

Reba nodded her agreement. "I agree. I've sent word to Sister Urillo via Portia. In the meantime we've got a problem. Sappo isn't going to tell us where Pong is, and Scavenger Jack is dead, so what do we do now?"

There was a long silence during which they watched McCade's smoke drift on the heavy air. It was Neem who finally spoke.

"In spite of your best efforts you humans have dropped

the globe. So it's time for an Il Ronnian to step in and save the day.''

"Oh, really?" Reba asked. "And how will you accomplish that, O wizened one?"

Neem smiled a superior smile. "It just so happens that Tin Town boasts a Class III Il Ronnian intelligence operation. I think it likely that our operatives will know where Pong is . . . or where to start looking. I suggest we drop in and ask them."

Twenty-two

McCADE WAS SURPRISED. It seemed hard to believe that the Il Ronn had spies on Tin Town. Subjugated races spying for the Il Ronn yes, human traitors yes, but the Il Ronn themselves? No.

For one thing there was the obvious physical differences. How could an Il Ronnian possibly pass for human? Or vice versa? Sure, there was Neem's disguise, but he couldn't get away with that forever. No, Il Ronnian spies didn't seem possible. Nonetheless that's exactly what Neem wanted them to believe.

McCade came to a stop as a pink robot trundled out to block Neem's path. A woman appeared next to it. She wore a skin suit and a rather tired expression.

"Step through my door, tall, dark, and handsome," she said. "I've got what you're looking for."

"I doubt that very much," Neem replied dryly as he sidestepped the robo pimp. "You're not my type."

McCade smiled as the woman made a rude gesture. Wouldn't she be surprised to see Neem in the nude!

Lights strobed, people swirled, and mind-numbing noise

assailed their ears as they threaded their way through the crowd.

Neem was his usual self, but Reba was a bit grumpy, as if Scavenger Jack's death was a personal affront to her honor. Having been unable to cheer her up, McCade decided to let her sulk.

Level six of Alpha Section was located at the opposite end of the habitat from the House of Yarl and that's where Neem was taking them. A high-speed monorail whisked them the length of the original barge and deposited them in a somewhat gaudy station.

Like the rest of Tin Town, Alpha Section was a sort of capitalistic free-for-all, governed by nothing more elaborate than the law of supply and demand.

Though McCade wondered how Il Ronnians could survive undetected, it was clear that spies would thrive on Tin Town's laissez-faire system of government and profit from the information that changed hands here. Maybe, just maybe, Neem was right.

Neem claimed that he'd been specially briefed by the chief of Il Ronnian intelligence during McCade's last days on Imantha. Though Neem was not normally privy to classified information, the Council of One Thousand had anticipated the possibility that he might need some help and granted him a special dispensation.

Not eager to reveal the extent of the Il Ronnian intelligence network to a human, Teeb had ordered Neem to keep the information secret unless forced to do otherwise. Or so Neem claimed.

McCade wasn't so sure. In retrospect, Neem had been a lot more competent than any college professor had a right to be. First he'd extricated himself from a bad situation on Spin, then he'd shown up to rescue McCade from the pirates, and now he was beheading people right and left. Yes, McCade decided, Neem will bear watching.

They rounded a corner and found themselves on the edge of a circular plaza. Shops and restaurants faced the plaza, which wasn't flat, but fell in levels toward a circular stage.

At the moment four jugglers were busy tossing daggers at one another, catching them and pretending not to, thrilling the audience with a series of close calls.

Neem glanced at his wrist term. "Come on. We've got some time to kill." The Il Ronnian made his way down the steps and McCade followed with a disgruntled Reba tagging along behind.

Neem slid sideways down a half-filled aisle. The Il Ronnian seemed to step on every third foot, leaving McCade and Reba to make his apologies.

The jugglers had finished with the knives and were moving on to Rath snakes by the time all three of them were seated. Rath snakes are somewhat irritable to start with, and the process of being thrown around did nothing to improve their tempers.

As they flew through the air the reptiles twisted every which way, hoping to sink their poisonous fangs into an arm or hand. But the jugglers were a blur, anticipating every move, whipping the snakes back and forth like pieces of green rope.

Then something went wrong. One of the jugglers missed a catch. A squirming Rath snake soared out over the audience and started to fall.

The crowd let out a collective gasp and people scrambled to get out of the way. All except for a man in baggy coveralls. He seemed frozen in place as the snake fell toward him, his mouth hanging open in stupefied amazement, his hands opening and closing as if unsure of what to do.

McCade's hand went toward his blaster, but he knew it was hopeless. By the time he drew and fired, the Rath snake would already have its fangs in the man's flesh.

Then just as the reptile was about to land in his lap, the man stood, snatched the snake out of midair, and threw it back.

A juggler caught it, tossed it into the air, and the crowd realized they'd been had. There was loud applause as the fifth juggler took a bow, stripped off his coveralls to reveal a colorful costume, and hurried down to join his friends onstage.

"Now would be the time to pass the hat," Reba remarked thoughtfully. "They should do pretty well."

"Chances are they've done pretty well already," McCade replied. "Look at the crowd they drew. I'll bet the stores fronting on the plaza pay them to perform."

McCade turned to Neem. "By the way, which store belongs to your friends?"

Neem chuckled. "None of them. My 'friends' as you call them are right in front of you."

McCade looked toward the stage. The jugglers had just activated thirty laser torches and were preparing to toss them around.

"You'd better have your eyes checked, Neem, the jugglers are human."

"They *look* human," Neem agreed, "but they aren't. They're cyborgs."

Il Ronnian cyborgs designed to look like humans? It couldn't be. But as McCade watched the jugglers he began to wonder. By now the laser torches were flashing through the air at incredible speed. Speed that defied human reflexes. And why not? If Neem was correct, the reflexes weren't human and never had been. They were wired, servo-controlled, and computer-assisted.

No wonder the jugglers were willing to throw Rath snakes around like so much rubber hose. A bite wouldn't even pierce their plastiflesh skin much less poison them. Much as he hated to admit it, the whole thing made sense. By posing as human jugglers, the Il Ronnian spies had a perfect excuse to travel around and poke their noses into all sorts of places. And given their skill people probably begged them to come!

All of a sudden the enormity of it struck home. There could be hundreds, even thousands, of Il Ronnian spies roaming the Empire sucking up secrets like so many vacuum cleaners. Swanson-Pierce would go crazy!

But wait a minute, what would stop humans from doing

the same thing? Among the millions who'd seen him on Imantha had some been human? Fellow Terrans locked inside electro-mechanical bodies deep inside an enemy empire? If so, each and every one of them deserved a medal.

McCade's thoughts were swept away by the sound of loud applause. The jugglers took a series of quick bows, and when the audience started to leave, the cyborgs started to pack.

Neem motioned for McCade and Reba to stay put and pushed his way down toward the stage.

"Where's Neem headed?"

"You're going to find this hard to believe," McCade replied, "but according to Neem the jugglers are Il Ronnian spies."

As McCade explained Reba's eyes got larger. When he was finished she shook her head and laughed out loud.

"Well, I'll be damned. It makes a lot of sense now that I think about it. I'll bet both sides have been at it for years. Sister Urillo will have a fit! She'll see Il Ronnian spies under every bed."

McCade nodded and felt through his pockets for a cigar. The best he could find was broken in two. He stuck the longer half between his teeth and puffed it into life.

Down on the stage Neem had just sealed some sort of agreement with a very human handshake. McCade blew smoke toward the deck and watched Neem climb the stairs. Strange though it seemed, things were looking up.

Twenty-three

MORRIS SAPPO HAD spent a lot of money to make himself both comfortable and safe. Not satisfied with what Tin Town had to offer, he'd commissioned a sort of annex, a blister on the habitat's hull built to his own specifications.

According to rumor, Sappo's quarters were luxurious beyond compare. A farm boy once, Sappo hated Tin Town's small spaces and hungered for the vast skies of Regor II. In order to satisfy his craving for openness he covered his home with transparent duraplast. If he couldn't have the blue sky of his boyhood, he'd have the heavens beyond.

Having started with the stars themselves as decorations, Sappo was challenged to do them justice. Fantastic holograms, each one a work of art, rippled across his walls in harmony with Sappo's moods. Expensive furniture, much of it specially crafted for his small frame, dotted his combination office and living room. And water swirled this way and that beneath his feet, trapped there between two layers of duraplast, tinted with multicolored dyes and programmed to match the walls.

That's what rumor said anyway, but if their plan worked,

McCade would soon know for himself. Two standard days had passed since the Il Ronnian cyborgs had performed in the plaza. Now they were about to take part in a performance of a different kind—an assault on Sappo's private quarters.

Neem had anticipated a certain amount of resentment, even resistance, from the cyborgs, and was surprised by their cheerful cooperation.

Unknown to Neem, or so he claimed, Teeb had provided him with an authorization code so powerful that the cyborgs regarded him as the direct embodiment of the governing council.

In addition, they were astounded to discover that Neem was running around the human empire protected by nothing more than a flimsy disguise. So they not only jumped to do his bidding but hung on his every word as well.

While McCade and Reba found this quite amusing, poor Neem was quite taken aback and spent a lot of time ordering the cyborgs to treat him just like anyone else.

Unfortunately the cyborgs took his entreaties as a form of divine humility and reacted by elevating him to new heights. From Neem's point of view the whole thing was quite disconcerting.

But regardless of their attitude toward Neem, the cyborgs were quite competent. This became clear during the two days spent planning and preparing the raid. Each was a specialist recruited from the various branches of the Il Ronnian armed forces. With but one expectation, all had been severely injured during combat prior to recruitment into the Cyborg Corps.

As Leeb, the explosives expert, put it, "The decision becomes relatively simple once your body is almost completely destroyed."

The single exception was their leader Ceex. Ceex was a professional intelligence officer so devoted to his job that he'd voluntarily given up a perfectly healthy body to become a cyborg.

In Neem's opinion Ceex was a few planets short of a full system, but since the anthropologist was a head case himself, this seemed like a case of the pot calling the kettle black. Still, it did seem as if Ceex had taken patriotism a step too far.

But looney or not, once Ceex understood the situation, he wasted little time in coming up with a plan. He didn't know where Pong was but felt sure that Morris Sappo did. The two men were often seen together and it was common knowledge that Sappo routinely purchased large quantities of Pong's stolen goods.

Given that, and given the limited amount of time to work with, Ceex suggested the direct approach. Bypass Sappo's security, break into his quarters, and force him to tell whatever he knew.

It wasn't very subtle, but given the stakes involved, and the need to get moving, McCade was in no mood for subtlety.

A scouting mission by Leeb and weapons expert Keeg confirmed what everyone already knew. Sappo's quarters would be a tough nut to crack. He had guards everywhere. In addition there were elaborate alarm systems, robotic sensors, and automatic defense systems.

"What you're saying is that the front door's locked," McCade had responded thoughtfully.

"Correct," Keeg agreed. He had the appearance of a pleasant young man with blond hair. "The back door, however, looks a good deal more promising."

"The back door?"

Keeg grinned an extremely human grin. "Yes. From what Leeb and I saw, Sappo's security system assumes that intruders will come from *inside* Tin Town. And a quick scouting trip on the surface of the hull confirmed it. Oh, there's plenty of nasty stuff out there as well, but compared with the inside approach, the outside is wide open."

And so it was agreed that they'd attack Sappo's quarters from the surface of Tin Town's hull. Now they were in place and about to venture out onto the habitat's surface. The cyborgs waited patiently while McCade, Neem, and Reba checked their space armor.

When all three had given Ceex the thumbs-up, he palmed the lock and waited for the atmosphere to hiss away. This particular lock was just outside the edge of Sappo's security systems.

Like the rest of the cyborgs, Ceex wore no body armor. He didn't need any. Outside of his brain and spinal cord he didn't have any biological parts. His internal life-support system would keep both organs well oxygenated and protect them from physical trauma. Still, it seemed strange to see a man step outside without a suit.

Tin Town's surface was a labyrinth of harsh shadows. A cooling fin towered off to McCade's right. It was back lit by a large sign that read MAMA SALDO'S SHIPYARD and threw triangles of black across the habitat's gleaming hull as it flashed on and off.

An automatic weapons turret swiveled around and around to McCade's left, its sensors probing the heavens for some sign of hostility, its twin-energy projectors waiting patiently for the order to fire.

And up ahead a maze of ducts, sensor housings, and clustered pipe waited to slow them down. And beyond that McCade could see the Beta end of the spindle, blazing with light and hanging against the stars like a big silver ball.

Movement caught McCade's eye and he looked up to see a sleek freighter fire her steering jets, pause, and slide out of sight beyond the hull's horizon.

The cyborgs drifted between the obstacles like so many ghosts. Their infrared beams probed the darkest corners, their transceivers sampled all the radio traffic in the immediate vicinity, and their optical scanners watched for signs of movement.

But even cyborgs are fallible, a lesson all would learn a few minutes later.

Although Tin Town didn't have any government as such, it did offer a number of police companies, one of which offered robo surveillance service. The service was designed to discourage unauthorized excursions over portions of privately owned hull. And the key to the service were the small globular devices called robo sentries. They didn't have much brain, but they bristled with weapons and flew preprogrammed patterns over the hull's surface.

The robo sentries were launched and retrieved via large pipes that passed through Tin Town's hull at various points. Although McCade didn't see the silver ball sail out of a pipe behind him, he did see it burn a hole through the rearmost cyborg's back and splash blue fire against the hull beyond.

The cyborg, an individual named Seeo, staggered but managed to stay upright. A mist of white fluid rose to envelope him.

McCade's energy rifle spat blue light as the robo sentry spun right and tried to line up on Neem. Though heavily armed, the robots didn't carry much armor and the silver ball exploded in an orange flash.

For a moment Neem was showered with pieces of hot metal and plastic. Then they lost their inertia and slowly drifted away, each one reflecting tiny shards of light.

"Sorry about that." It was Ceex's voice in McCade's helmet. "It looks like the cyborg's out of the bag."

A part of McCade's mind registered the joke. The rest was busy staying alive. The robo sentry had sent out a distress signal before it died and now silver balls were flocking to the spot like sharks to a feeding frenzy.

McCade took cover behind some sort of metal housing and began to pick them off one at a time. First he'd compute a robot's trajectory, next he'd pick a spot just ahead of it, and then he'd squeeze the trigger. Nine times out of ten the robot disappeared in a flash of orange flame. The others joined in and pretty soon robo sentries were popping like so many party balloons.

The battle was not entirely one-sided however. While McCade and the others fought off most of the swarming globes, five or six managed to surround Seeo and soon finished him off. Like the professional he was, Seeo died without uttering a sound.

Seconds later his life-support system confirmed his death,

triggered his built-in demo charge, and blew up. Two of the silver balls disappeared along with Seeo's body.

"Damn." Reba's voice sounded hollow in McCade's helmet.

"Yeah," he replied. "Damn."

"Let's move," Ceex said, sounding like every noncom McCade had ever heard. "Sappo's quarters are just ahead."

They were running now, a sort of fast shuffle that ate up the distance but maintained their contact with Tin Town's hull. They knew that each passing second would bring more and more opposition and give Sappo's household security troops that much more time to get ready.

McCade welcomed the movement. After all the deception and delay, it felt good to *do* something for a change. Even if the something was dangerous as hell. His muscles strained, his pulse pounded, and the ragged sound of his own breathing filled his helmet.

Every now and then another robo sentry would appear, loose off a bolt of energy, and disappear in a flash of light as someone blew it away. Once you knew about them they weren't that hard to handle.

"We've got security troops up here," Ceex said grimly. "Get ready to take some heat."

McCade climbed over a low pipe and saw a strange sight waiting up ahead. Four members of Sappo's household troops had exited through his private lock and come face-to-face with the II Ronnian cyborgs. But Sappo's troops didn't *know* that the men who faced them were cyborgs. And not knowing they stood frozen in place wondering how humans could enter a vacuum and stay alive.

None of them lived long enough to find out. One after another they fell as the strange apparitions shot them down. Two died without firing, the third got off a single shot, and the fourth killed Keeg a fraction of a second before Leeb drilled an energy beam through his visor. The cyborg blew up just as the man's visor shattered and the vacuum sucked him out through the hole in his helmet.

It wasn't a pretty sight, but McCade didn't have the time

to look. He was too busy helping Leeb place explosives around Sappo's private lock. A few seconds later and the cyborg was pushing McCade toward cover.

They were just barely behind a boxy piece of duct work when the charges went off. McCade peeked around the corner just in time to see the outer hatch fly off its hinges and spin into space.

Neem and Reba were right behind him as he and Leeb dashed for the lock.

"We've got more troops out here," Ceex warned. "Geev and I will hold them off while you secure the lock."

"Roger," McCade replied.

The tunnel had decompressed as they blew the hatch, but there was another lock just fifty feet in. It had been placed there in case the first lock failed.

"Just a sec and I'll blow it," Leeb said, reaching for his demolitions bag.

"Whoa," McCade ordered. "If we aren't careful, we could decompress Sappo's entire area. He won't be much good to us if he's dead."

McCade palmed the door and it slid open. It seemed all the security measures had been lavished on the outer door, leaving this one unprotected.

McCade chinned his radio. "The lock is secured, Ceex. Time to join us."

The cyborg arrived a few seconds later. His energy rifle had disappeared along with his right arm. White hydraulic fluid spurted from the stump and half his face was burned away. "Sorry I'm late. Geev won't be coming."

McCade remembered Geev's dark plastiflesh, his flashing brown eyes, and his ready smile. He hoped that whatever Sappo had to say would be worth the price, and wondered if that was possible.

The outer door closed, air hissed into the lock, and the inner door cycled open a few minutes later. They were all on the deck with weapons ready, but nothing could have prepared them for the hail of lead and coherent energy that reached out to greet them.

It was Reba who saved the day when she stood up and lobbed a grenade down the corridor. She was still standing there waiting for the grenade to go off when Neem reached up and jerked her down.

The grenade turned the other end of the corridor into a slaughter house and Neem threw another just to make sure. Like the first one it went off with a deafening roar. They waited for a few moments, but there were no signs of life, so one by one they all got up.

All that is but Leeb. A piece of shrapnel had lanced down through his chest ripping his life-support system apart and destroying his motor control subprocessor.

McCade bent to help him, but Ceex pulled him away. "He's gone, Sam, and if you stay here, he'll take you with him."

They were forty feet down the corridor when Leeb blew up. The explosion made a dull thumping sound and no one chose to look back.

Their entrance into Sappo's quarters was almost anticlimactic. As the door hissed open they were ready for anything, but rather than armor-clad troops a domestic robot rolled forward to greet them. Its synthesized voice was stern and unyielding.

"Please leave. Your presence is not wanted here. I will summon help if necessary. Please leave . . ."

The robot never got to repeat its warning because Reba put her hand blaster up against its metal forehead and pulled the trigger. The beam of blue energy went right through the thin metal and out the other side.

On the far side of the room a tank filled with Nuerillium air fresh shattered into a thousand pieces, freeing its multicolored captives to flutter about the room.

And what a room it was. If anything the rumors had understated its elegance. Overhead the vast sweep of the starscape made the room seem huge. The holos added to that impression, wrapping the room in color and pulsating to the beat of the exotic music that floated through the air. And water eddied and swirled beneath their boots looking like marble brought to life. The overall effect was beautiful but cold like a piece of sculpture that is seen and not touched.

"All right," McCade said grimly. "Sappo's in here somewhere. Spread out and find him."

No one had taken more than a couple of steps before a section of holo rippled and a man stepped out. He was small, carefully dressed, and as far as McCade could tell completely unarmed. He wore an amused, almost arrogant expression, and frowned when he saw the air fish fluttering around the room.

"I don't know who you people are but you're certainly destructive. If this is an attempt to rob me, I'm afraid you'll be sadly disappointed. I keep my cash and other valuables somewhere else."

"No," Neem answered as he walked across the room toward Sappo. "This is not an attempt to steal your stupid possessions. What we want is knowledge. Knowledge stored in your brain. And we'll do whatever's necessary to get it."

Sappo became visibly nervous as Neem drew closer. "My brain? Knowledge? What do you want?"

The black plastic of Neem's visor was only inches away when he spoke. "We want the location of a man. A friend of yours by the name of Mustapha Pong. Give us what we want and you'll live."

Sappo was scared now. He took a step backward. "You don't understand . . . I can't . . . Pong would kill me."

Neem reached up to remove his helmet. As it came away he said, "No, *you* don't understand. If you *don't* tell, I'll kill you. I'll strip your skin off one inch at a time until you pray for death with every breath you take."

Sappo took one look at Neem's distorted features and began to scream.

Twenty-four

A WEEK HAD passed since their assault on Sappo's quarters. Now *Pegasus* was closing in on asteroid FA 6789-X. It was better known as the Dump, and from what McCade could see via his long-range optics, the name fit. FA 6789-X had once served as an Imperial supply dump, a staging area for some long-forgotten mission, an airless lump of rock to be used and then abandoned.

A long list of temporary residents had come and gone since then, including a succession of miners, an eccentric loner or two, and most recently Mustapha Pong. Or so Morris Sappo claimed.

And McCade was inclined to believe him. For one thing Sappo was scared, and for another he was sitting in ship's lounge where Neem could reach out and touch him, something the human would do anything to avoid.

Sappo had some rather deep-seated religious beliefs stemming from his childhood on Regor II. There his parents had attempted to beat an understanding of good and evil into his scrawny little body, and even though they'd failed, they had managed to warp his mind. So even though Sappo knew that Neem wasn't the devil, the Il Ronnian's demonic appearance still turned him into a babbling idiot. And babbling idiots can be extremely cooperative.

Thanks to a cooperative Sappo, they'd been able to lift from Tin Town without interference, and without payment for the considerable damage they'd caused. So when Sappo said that Pong made regular use of the Dump, McCade believed him.

The only problem was that McCade couldn't tell if the pirate was in residence or not. McCade spoke without taking his eyes off the screen. "Reba, cycle through the sensors one more time."

"Okay," she replied. "But it won't do much good. There's so much junk on the ground that you could hide the Imperial fleet down there."

Reba was right, of course. The original supply dump had centered around a cluster of domes. When the navy pulled out, all sorts of junk was left behind. Broken-down crawlers, gantries, and other less identifiable chunks of equipment lay all over the place. As the years passed, other tenants had added their debris to the pile so that a jungle of wrecked ships, scrap metal, and other junk filled a good-sized crater.

As a result there was enough metal on Dump to put all of McCade's metal detectors onto eternal alert. On top of that were radiation leaks from junked drives, a lot of vague static, and residual heat emanating from God knows what. It could mean nothing or everything. There was no way to tell.

Reba looked up from her sensors. "Sorry, Sam. There's too much input. If Pong's there, I can't pick his ship out of the background clutter."

McCade nodded and stuck an unlit cigar between his teeth. He could land and risk falling into a trap or stay a safe distance away and wait for something to happen. A day? A week? A month? It made little difference because he couldn't afford to use any time at all. Unless he found the Vial of Tears, and found it damn soon, entire planets would begin to burn.

"Strap in, everybody. We're going down."

It was a simple approach. FA 6789-X had a nice predictable orbit with just the right amount of spin to generate light gravity.

The problem was where to land. The crater was so full of junk that there wasn't much open space left. That seemed to suggest a landing outside the crater's perimeter, but if he did that, *Pegasus* would stick out like a Zord at a Finthian tree dance. And if Pong returned, he'd see the little ship and destroy it. That left the crater junk or no junk. It might be a tight fit, but once down *Pegasus* would fade into the background. In fact, they could lay an ambush for Pong if that seemed advisable.

As the asteroid grew larger in his viewscreens, McCade swung *Pegasus* to the right and used his repellors to skim across the crater. "Keep a sharp lookout, Reba. Let me know if you see anything funny."

But Reba was silent as they passed over the forest of junk. Light dusted the tops of things and sparkled off the billions of dust motes that were stirred up by the ship's repellors. But outside of the ship itself nothing moved or gave McCade reason to run.

McCade put *Pegasus* down in the shadow of a huge ore processor. It was a tight fit between that and a pile of metal scaffolding, but he made it. He used the ship's sensors to take one last look around. Nothing. If Pong were present, surely he'd have reacted by now.

McCade released his harness, stuck the cigar in a pocket, and followed Reba out of the control room.

Neem, Sappo, and Ceex were already in the lounge when they arrived, so the tiny space was full to overflowing. Now that they were down McCade was anxious to look around.

"All right. With the exception of Ceex, I want everyone suited up. Yes, Sappo, that means you. If anything unpleasant happens to us while we're out there, it's gonna happen to you too."

"Ceex, I want you to stay aboard *Pegasus* and man the weapons systems. If anything moves, blast it."

"Maybe he should "Il Ronnian" the weapons systems instead," Neem suggested with a smile.

"Give me a break, Neem. That okay with you, Ceex?"

The cyborg nodded. Half his face was a mass of melted plastic that dripped downward like wax from a candle. The other half wore a twisted smile.

They'd done the best they could for him, but the truth was that his injuries required the attentions of a fully equipped cyberlab, and an Il Ronnian cyberlab at that. But Ceex had insisted that he be allowed to come along, and this way he'd be useful without slowing them down.

"All right then," McCade said. "Let's suit up and take a look around. I want everyone to carry an extra oxygen supply and a blast rifle. There's no telling what we might run into out there and we may want to stay awhile."

Forty-five minutes later McCade scrambled down to the ground and took a look around. Huge pieces of equipment formed a metal maze on every side. There were thousands of hiding places and everyone of them could harbor an ambush. But why bother? McCade thought to himself. If Pong's here, we would have seen him by now.

They had chosen the original domes as their destination. According to Sappo, that's where Pong stored some of his loot between raids, and if they decided to lay an ambush for him, that would be the place to do it.

McCade and Reba took the point with Sappo following along behind and Neem bringing up the rear. Constrained as he was by McCade's leg shackles, Sappo couldn't move very fast but that was fine. The rest of them were loaded down with extra oxygen and weapons so they weren't moving very fast either. But the light gravity helped as did a certain amount of fear.

It was spooky in and among the junk. Their movements carried them from heavy shadow to bright sunlight and back again. It took very little imagination to turn twisted pieces of metal into homicidal aliens.

Once, McCade thought that he saw a weapons turret on a junked shuttle turn to track them, but when he stopped to look again, he saw that it was just the way the light had moved across its surface.

And twice he thought he saw movement, first between two hydroponics tanks, and then through the canopy of an old crane.

On both occasions he used his radio to ask Ceex for confirmation, but the cyborg hadn't seen anything and swore that all of his sensors were clear.

Over the years a number of natural paths had evolved in and between the larger pieces of junk. These were well marked by crawler tracks, but it was impossible to tell how recently they'd been used. Without the effects of weather to wash them away, many were probably twenty or thirty years old.

Finally· the domes loomed up ahead. One had been crushed by a badly piloted ore barge years before, one had been stripped for use somewhere else, and three appeared to be in reasonably good shape.

McCade and Reba approached the first of these while Neem and Sappo hung back. Its surface was checkered with solar cells, heat exchangers, and other less-obvious equipment. Crude patches were visible here and there where someone had modified the dome for a particular use and someone else had come along to restore it.

They circled the dome by carefully working their way along the wall until they reached the main door. It was wide open. Stepping inside McCade saw endless rows of empty shelves. There was something about them, something about the used pallets scattered here and there, and the multitude of tracks that ran every which way that suggested recent use. Had Pong emptied the warehouse? And if so, why?

"Sam! Reba! You'd better get out here!" The voice belonged to Neem.

They came at a fast trot and the moment he got outside McCade saw the problem. It was rather hard to miss. Though not huge, a light cruiser is a large ship and this one was hovering about a hundred feet over the crater. It was roughly triangular in shape and was covered with weapons turrets, torpedo launchers, and a host of other installations. Though too large to land on most planets, the absence of an atmosphere and the asteroid's lighter gravity permitted the ship to come in close.

"The damn thing was hiding in the junk on the far side of the crater," Neem said grimly. "One moment it wasn't there and the next moment it was."

McCade chinned his mike. "Don't try it, Ceex, you don't have a . . ." but he could have saved his breath.

Ceex opened up with everything he had, but it was like a zit bug taking on an Envo Beast. *Pegasus* was heavily armed for a ship her size, but the larger ship's defensive screen shrugged off her puny attack as if it hadn't even happened and then responded in kind.

Huge energy projectors burped blue light and *Pegasus* exploded into a million pieces. They seemed to fall forever due to the asteroid's light gravity and hit with exaggerated force.

McCade simply stood there completely helpless while his ship and a trusted comrade died in front of his eyes.

There was a burst of static in McCade's helmet followed by a voice he'd never heard before. "Welcome to the Dump. I'm Mustapha Pong, and unless you do exactly what I say, you will die."

Twenty-five

MCCADE HAD NEVER felt so helpless. The cruiser hung above them like some dark god, untouchable and omnipotent. With no atmosphere to conduct the sound of its repellors, the ship seemed all the more awesome and mysterious. Pong's voice filled McCade's helmet.

"Which one of you is Sam McCade? Raise your right arm."

McCade gulped and raised his right arm. There was little point in doing otherwise. If he chose to, Pong could turn the entire crater into a lake of molten metal.

A spear of white light flashed down to pin McCade against the ground. His heart stopped beating while he checked to make sure that he was still alive. With a sigh of relief he realized that it was nothing more than a spotlight.

"Good. Now tell me why you're here, and I warn you, McCade, do not waste my time. If you tell the truth, I will allow you and your friends to live. If you lie, or attempt to mislead me, I will know and our conversation will end rather abruptly. Do you understand?"

McCade understood. He understood that in spite of Pong's threats he should say as little as possible. The question was how much did Pong know? It couldn't be much or he'd have killed them by now. No, Pong was curious. He knew McCade was trying to find him and wanted to know why. He knew about Sappo's abduction but little else.

Thank God! If Pong knew about the vial and understood its value, he'd try to auction it off to the highest bidder, use it to extort money from the Il Ronn, or God knows what else.

McCade swallowed to lubricate a dry throat. "The answer's quite simple. The Brotherhood is offering five hundred thousand credits for your head, and I'm a little short on cash. Surrender peacefully and they'll go easy on you."

There was a long silence. And then, just as McCade was preparing to die, there was a loud laughter. When Pong spoke again, there was merriment in his voice.

"McCade, you're something else. You said the one thing that could save your life, and you said it with a certain amount of style. I like that. I like it so much that I'll let you live. Providing of course that you return my property."

McCade frowned and looked around helplessly. "What property is that? I wasn't aware that I had anything that belonged to you."

There was a burst of static followed by Pong's chuckle. "Oh, but you do. Unless I'm very much mistaken that's my good friend Morris standing over there, and while he's been a little too talkative of late, I'd like to offer him a ride home."

Another shaft of light lanced down to bathe Sappo in white. He waved enthusiastically to the ship and shuffled in a circle.

"Just follow the light, Morris, and a shuttle will pick you up."

The spotlight moved off toward the area where they'd landed and Sappo followed.

Something landed in McCade's stomach with a heavy thud. He chinned his mike. "Neem, Reba, move toward me and do it *now*."

Meanwhile Sappo hurried toward the white circle and came to a sudden halt when the light stopped moving. "That's far enough, Morris," Pong said sweetly. "I lied . . . and you know what that means."

Sappo looked around with desperate eyes searching for someplace to hide, someone to help. "Please, Mustapha, don't do this, they made me tell."

"Oh, really?" Pong asked quietly. "Are your eyes hanging down onto your cheeks? Are you walking on broken feet? Has every tooth been pulled from your lying mouth? If you can show me those injuries, I will spare you and tend your wounds with my own hands."

Sappo made no reply but tried to run. Due to his leg shackles he didn't get very far. A single burp of blue energy consumed Sappo, space armor and all, leaving nothing more than some scorched rock and a puddle of molten metal. In less than a second Sappo's shackles had been transformed into a marker for his grave.

"Good-bye, McCade. I hereby cede the Dump and all that it contains to you and your friends. Like Morris, it has ceased to be useful."

McCade chinned his mike. "In ten or twelve hours we'll run out of air."

Pong chuckled. "I said I'd let you live, but I didn't say for how long. Besides, as Morris just found out, I lie a lot. Bye."

And with that the cruiser drifted over the domes. Blue beams flashed down to burn huge holes in each structure. Then the ship engaged its main drives, lifted, and disappeared over the horizon.

"The bastard!" Reba shook her fist at the point where the ship had vanished.

McCade had never felt as depressed as he did at that

particular moment. They'd come close, damned close, and now it was over. Not just for them, but for the millions, the billions, who would die in the coming war. But before he could pursue that line of thought a strange voice filled his helmet.

"Testing . . . testing . . . can you hear me? Hello, can anybody hear me?"

"I can hear you," McCade replied. "Who are you? Where are you?"

"I call myself Henry," the voice replied. "Although my manual says I'm a NAVCOMP IN7808/L. But that seemed so impersonal I decided to name myself after a great navigator called Henry."

"It's a nice name," McCade agreed. "Although Henry had a tendency to hang around Portugal while other folks did the actual navigating."

McCade looked around and tried to spot where the voice might be coming from. "So you're a robot?"

"Certainly not!" Henry replied, obviously offended. "A NAVCOMP IN7808/L is a far cry from some piece of animated junk. I'm a top of the line navigational computer, and proud of it. Pong didn't like me, and well, I thought we could be friends."

"Sounds good to me," McCade replied. "Where are you? Let's shake on it."

"Right here," Henry said as a birdlike creature stalked out of the shadows. Something about its jerky walk reminded McCade of the movement he'd spotted earlier.

Henry had a cylindrical body and three skinny legs. Two arms stuck out at odd angles, one of which boasted a three-fingered hand, the other being equipped with some sort of complicated tool. He had a long flexible neck that extended out and up from his cylindrical body to a ball-like head. An antenna stuck straight out in front to suggest a beak and thereby cement Henry's resemblance to a bird.

McCade extended his right hand and found Henry's grip to be surprisingly delicate. "I'm Sam McCade. That's Reba, and the taller one is Neem. It's a pleasure to meet you, Henry.''

''Likewise I'm sure,'' Henry replied politely. ''Hello, Reba, hello, Neem. I'm sorry about your ship. Had I known you were good people I would have warned you, but I thought you were part of Pong's security forces. They try to hunt me down every now and then.''

''They tried to hunt you down?'' Reba asked. ''Whatever for?''

Henry's head drooped toward his metal chest. ''They want to terminate me. I was the navigational computer aboard Pong's ship until I made a mistake and miscalculated a hyperspace jump. No one was hurt, and everything turned out just fine, but Pong was angry and had me junked. He said I was stupid, but it wasn't my fault. I told the maintenance tech to check a short in my number four logic sequencer, but he said it could wait.''

''So Pong threw you on the scrap heap?''

''That's right,'' Henry replied, ''but I didn't stay there. I was wearing my control console body when they threw me outside. It includes my head and one articulated limb that I use for routine maintenance.''

''I still don't understand why they'd try and terminate you,'' Reba said. ''Why bother?''

''I don't know,'' Henry replied simply. ''I guess Pong thought I'd die out here and when I didn't he got mad. Anyway I managed to drag myself into this labyrinth of junk where I went to work on building myself a new body. Bodies actually, since I now have three, each being dedicated to a different purpose. They tend to be a bit asymmetrical since I cobbled them together from junk, but appearances aren't everything. This is the body I use for working on the ship. What do you think?'' Henry turned himself around like a model on a runway.

''Very nice,'' McCade said approvingly. ''Did you say something about a ship?'' He tried to conceal his eagerness but failed.

''Ship? Oh, yes, the ship. Well, a NAVCOMP IN7808/

L isn't worth much without a ship, so I've been repairing an old freighter I found. I can't imagine how they got it here. After I revived the ship's NAVCOMP, I learned it was retarded. Poor thing, I put it to sleep.''

"I see," McCade replied, not quite sure whether he approved or not. "How long before your ship's ready to lift?"

"With some help I could do it in three or four standards, without help a couple of weeks, a month max."

"If we helped, would you give us a lift?"

"I'd give you a lift even if you didn't help," Henry replied cheerfully. "Though partially sentient, I'm also programmed to help humans, especially where matters of navigation are concerned."

"Excellent," McCade said, his spirits rising. "You've got yourself a crew."

Reba cleared her throat. "Aren't you forgetting something, Sam? You know, the stuff we breathe?"

"Oxygen?" Henry asked. "I don't use the stuff myself, but there's lots of it around." He gestured toward the surrounding junk with his three-fingered hand. "I come across it all the time."

"Well, then," Neem put in. "What are we waiting for? Let's repair the ship and haul rectum."

"Neem that's . . . oh, never mind," McCade said. "Let's do it."

It took three standard days of extremely hard work to ready the freighter for space, and even then the word "ready" was more optimism than reality.

McCade had never seen a ship exactly like it, and guessed the freighter was around a hundred years old. The last twenty or so of those years had been spent in the crater, and thanks to the surrounding vacuum, there'd been little or no deterioration to its hull.

She'd been chock full of number nine core drills when Henry found her. Someone had removed her drives, her weapons systems, and her old-fashioned hydroponics lab before converting her into a warehouse. But her hull was sound, her control systems were intact, and her auxiliary systems were still functional, so Henry went to work.

The first step was to unload the number nine core drills. Even with the asteroid's gravity this was quite a task since each drill weighed about eight hundred pounds. To deal with the situation Henry constructed a body small enough to negotiate the ship's narrow hatches but strong enough to pick up core drills four at a time. It looked like a cross between a fork lift and an all-terrain vehicle.

Once the core drills were removed Henry had systematically checked out every inch of the ship's wiring, run diagnostics on its antiquated subprocessors, and effected repairs wherever he could.

The next step was to find a drive, not just any drive, but one which would fit inside the little ship and could be linked to its ancient systems.

It took Henry the better part of a month to find the drive. And when he did it was in a lifeboat for a much larger ship. Like most lifeboats this one echoed the vessel it was built to serve. It was therefore almost as large as the freighter itself, and while it was twenty years newer, its systems were still compatible. Lifeboat design always seemed to lag behind everything else and for once that worked in someone's favor.

Tests proved that the drive was in fairly good shape but there was still a problem. The lifeboat was trapped under the wreckage of a mobile refinery that hadn't been mobile for ten years or more. And that's the problem that faced his new friends. How to move the refinery and get at the lifeboat's drive?

Difficult though the task was it could have been worse. They could move around freely now that Pong was gone and thanks to the accumulated junk there was plenty of stuff to work with.

First they went from wreck to wreck searching for, and finding, enough oxygen to last them a week or more. Once it was safely transferred to some portable storage tanks they were ready for the task at hand.

Both McCade and Neem were handy enough, but it was Reba who shouldered most of the load. She had a natural aptitude for things mechanical and it was she who repaired a large winch, ran more than two miles of durasteel cable through a series of improvised pulleys, and lifted the refinery clear.

And having done so, it was Reba who worked hand-in-hand with Henry to remove the lifeboat's drive and install it in the freighter.

McCade worked hard as well, but his tasks were more routine and left him time to think. And the more he thought, the more he believed that they still had a chance. If so, Henry would be the key.

But there was no point in discussing something like that until the ship was repaired.

Time passed, work went on, and final tests were run. Then as the drive hummed, and the main accumulators built up a charge, he popped the question.

The control room was the only part of the ship that would still hold an atmosphere and the three of them were sitting around with their helmets off. Since none of them had bathed in three days, the stink was terrible, but it felt good to escape the close confinement of their helmets. "Henry . . . I've got a question for you."

Henry had reverted to his smaller control module configuration and popped out of the console like a prairie dog coming out of its hole. He waved his single arm by way of a greeting. "Sure, Sam. What's up?"

"Does Pong have another base?"

"Yes he does," Henry said matter-of-factly. "His main base is in the heart of the Nakasoni Asteroid Belt. As a matter of fact this asteroid is located on the outer fringes of the great Nakasoni, which is why Pong used it. He needed a place where his business associates could come and go without learning the location of his home base."

Both Reba and Neem were suddenly paying attention. Neem was staring at Henry with an intensity that would've made a human somewhat nervous. "And the course to Pong's base . . . do you know it?"

Henry looked from Neem to McCade and back again. "Of course I know it . . . I'm a NAVCOMP IN7808/L, aren't I?"

Twenty-six

THERE WAS ZERO G inside the ship and that made the space sled easy to handle. McCade used small squirts of nitrogen to hold it in place as he waited for the hatch to open.

Outside, the Nakasoni Asteroid Belt stretched off for thousands of miles. And somewhere inside that vast drift of tumbling planetoids was Pong's secret base and, with any luck at all, the Vial of Tears.

McCade fought back the fatigue that threatened to roll over him and tongued another stim tab. This was number five, or was it six? It was hard to tell since the last few days had become one long blur of nonstop effort.

Sleep. He'd give anything to sleep, but sleep takes time, and time was slipping away. If they moved now, and if the plan worked, there was still a chance to recover the vial and prevent war.

Pong had done pretty well for himself since deserting the Brotherhood, but he'd made some mistakes too. The first was his decision to junk Henry, the second was his murder of Ceex, the third was his destruction of *Pegasus*, and the fourth was leaving McCade alive after committing the first three.

The hatch was wide open now. It served to frame the nearer asteroids and the starfield beyond. There were thousands of asteroids out there, ranging in size from small ones a mile or so in diameter, to larger specimens, some of which were five hundred times that size. And, just to keep things interesting, the asteroids were in constant motion relative to the sun and each other. So, if you didn't know the right way in, you could have one helluva a time finding your way out, and that wasn't all. There could be man-made hazards as well.

And that's why Henry and he were about to undertake a one NAVCOMP, one man scouting mission.

McCade chinned his mike. "Thanks for the lift. Don't bother to see us out, we know the way."

"That's a roger," Reba replied. "Neem sends his best. You two take care of yourselves. We'll meet you here in two standards, *Methuselah* willing."

Every ship should have a name, and since the freighter was old, more than a little crotchety, and very dependent on the goodwill of a supreme being, *Methuselah* had seemed perfect.

They had a plan although the word "plan" implied more order and logic than seemed apparent now. The heady realization that Henry could lead them to Pong's hidden base had been followed by an equally sobering discovery.

Henry knew how to get there, but he didn't remember what sort of defenses they might encounter, how many ships Pong had under his command, or anything else of military value.

As a partially sentient computer Henry was largely self-programming. That meant that while he had a predetermined "purpose" he was free to decide which areas of knowledge might be useful to the fulfillment of his mission and which wouldn't. And although Henry didn't like to admit it, the size of his memory was limited, and that forced him to make choices about what he'd remember and what he wouldn't.

And while he'd stored away the long strings of numbers necessary to find his way through the great Nakasoni to Pong's base, he hadn't seen fit to memorize whatever defenses lay along the path. On a large cruiser those matters were the province of other computers and not his concern.

So the decision was made to equip a modified space sled with extra oxygen that would allow McCade to scout the path into the asteroid belt. Henry would come along to guide him in and out again.

In the meantime Reba and Neem would take a short hyperspace jump to the nearest Imperial outpost and request help. Marshaling whatever forces were available, they would return and rendezvous with McCade and Henry. An assault on Pong's base would follow.

That was the plan anyway, and it might even work. If it didn't, McCade would spend eternity circling Cypra II with a few thousand asteroids for company.

Even though his part of the plan was fairly chancy, McCade wondered if Reba and Neem's was even worse. After all, a hyperspace shift involves a certain amount of risk even in a well-maintained ship, and *Methuselah* was anything but "well maintained."

One malfunction and they'd end up in a place that mathematicians were still arguing about. It wasn't a pleasant prospect.

When Reba spoke it seemed as if she were reading his mind. "If we don't show up, feel free to go ahead without us."

"Gee, thanks," McCade replied dryly.

"How's the Geezer?" The voice belonged to Henry. Having resurrected the freighter's moronic NAVCOMP, he'd named it "the Geezer." All the Geezer had to do was plot a single jump, but Henry still didn't trust him.

"The Geezer's lookin' good," Reba said. "He just cycled his self-diagnostics and says he's in great shape. Says he'll be plotting jumps long after you've been recycled into a coffee pot."

Henry gave a snort of derision but lapsed into silence as

McCade squeezed both handgrips and launched the tiny sled into the vastness of space. After putting some distance between himself and the ship, McCade released the left grip for a second and then both grips together. The sled turned left and drifted forward on inertia alone.

Methuselah was a black shadow against the stars beyond. "I'm clear."

"Roger," Reba replied. "Take care, Sam. We'll see you soon."

McCade watched as Reba fed power to the ship's single drive and *Methuselah* merged with the blackness of space.

A vast loneliness welled up inside McCade as he watched the ship disappear. Without his companions he was smaller somehow, the smallest and least significant microorganism in the vast ocean of space, and almost completely helpless.

It was Henry who snapped him out of it. The NAVCOMP was attired in a modified version of his control console body. He still resembled a round metal ball with a single articulated limb, but he'd added a small solar collector to augment his battery power, and some wiring to access the sled's primitive control system. He was strapped down beneath McCade's seat.

Henry would take the controls from here on out, freeing McCade to observe and watch for trouble. One of five sleds they'd found stored away in a ruined dome, theirs was designed for external ship repairs or ship-to-ship errands. As such it had no hull, no weapons, and no padding for the skeletal seats.

McCade shifted his weight and tried to find a more comfortable position. His skin was raw where the suit had rubbed against it for the last four days, he had a nonstop urge to scratch places he couldn't reach, and even after the stim tab he was still bone-tired.

"Sam, if you'll release the controls, I'll take over."

McCade released the controls. "You've got the con, Henry . . . take it away."

And Henry did. Using the sled's rudimentary sensors to see where he was going, the NAVCOMP brought the sled up to half speed and headed into the asteroid belt.

The ride quickly became one of the most exhilarating and terrifying trips of McCade's life. He'd taken a number of short trips into open space, some on sleds and some in armor alone. But he'd never gone farther than a few miles and help had always been seconds away. Now he was setting off on a journey of hundreds, maybe thousands, of miles, and doing it through a twisting, turning maze of asteroids.

Although miles apart, many of the asteroids were in sight of each other, and that added to the sensation of movement as McCade passed between them. Time lost all its meaning as the hours rolled swiftly by and the readouts for his oxygen tanks steadily unwound.

Distant specks of reflected light grew larger and larger until they blocked the starfield beyond and hurtled by a few hundred feet to one side or the other. Bright sunlight slid across the surface of slowly tumbling asteroids creating an endless dance of light and dark. It was beautiful, so beautiful that McCade became lost in the majesty of it, and almost missed the first sensor station.

All he had was the momentary impression of light glinting off a metal surface and then it was gone. "Slow down, Henry, and make a note that we just passed some sort of sensor emplacement. Chances are there's more up ahead."

And there were. Moving more cautiously now, Henry eased his way between the asteroids, giving McCade a chance to spot the sensors. They came at regular intervals and each installation looked the same. They consisted of a metal box crammed with electronics, a flowerlike solar collector, and a thicket of shiny antennas.

Thanks to the sensors Pong would receive a running progress report on any ships approaching or leaving his base. When the attack came he'd have lots of warning. It couldn't be helped though. There were way too many emplacements for McCade to destroy by himself, and even if he found a way to do it, the act itself would be a warning.

There was also the possibility that the sensors had picked up the sled and were tracking it all the way. But the sled had very little mass, no radio signature, and its nitrogen-gas propulsion system didn't put out any heat.

So, unless he began a series of loops and barrel rolls, the sensors would probably ignore him. Since this was an asteroid belt, pieces of flying junk were a centime a dozen.

Suddenly the asteroid belt began to close in on itself. Now the rocks were only miles apart, and even though Henry had slowed the sled to a virtual crawl, they seemed to flash by at incredible speed.

Then McCade saw them, one, two, three weapons emplacements up ahead, all positioned to place ships in a cross fire as they came through the narrow passage.

Speaking in a quiet monotone, McCade began to feed Henry information. The NAVCOMP would put it together with the relevant navigational coordinates and produce a detailed report on Pong's defenses.

"The outer ring of weapons emplacements appear to be automated," McCade noted, "since there's no sign of associated living quarters. There could be concealed living quarters somewhere underground of course, but I don't think so. There's none of the junk that seems to pile up when sentients are about.

"Now we're passing through the narrowest part of the passageway. I don't see any fortifications here. That makes sense because opposing emplacements would end up firing on each other.

"Now things are loosening up a bit, wait a minute there's something shiny up ahead; uh-oh, I see emplacements on all the surrounding asteroids. Some are controlled by automatics but some appear to be manned.

"The passageway is wider now and opens up a few miles ahead. There's a large sphere-shaped open space with densely packed asteroids forming the outer surface. In toward the center I see a few free-floating asteroids, and there, right in the middle, I see a reflective surface. It's big, not as big as the larger asteroids, but damned big just the same.

"We're getting closer now . . . I'll be damned . . . it's a ship! Not just *any* ship but a liner. And not just any liner

but the *Earth Star*! I'd recognize that H-shaped hull anywhere. It seems she wasn't lost in hyperspace like everyone
thought. Pong got her instead. God knows what happened
to her passengers and crew.

"This is good enough, Henry . . . put us alongside that
chunk of rock over there. This close in they'll be watching
the smaller stuff too. Good. Now, starting with the *Earth
Star* and working my way around to the right, I see all sorts
of ships. I see a DE, three heavy cruisers, two light cruisers,
another DE, six, make that seven destroyers, two armed
freighters, an ore barge, two hulks, and a tug.

"Based on visible running lights and jet flares I'd say
there's plenty of small craft running around and some of
them are probably armed. There's no way to tell if he's got
any interceptors loaded aboard the *Earth Star* or the cruisers
but chances are that he does. In addition, I see that one of
the nearby island type asteroids has been equipped as a Class
C dockyard. I think there's a ship in the yard but I can't
tell what kind. Got all that, Henry?"

"I've got it, Sam. What now?"

"Now we turn around and get while the getting's good."

Henry obediently turned the sled away from the free-
floating chunk of rock and headed back toward the passageway. They hadn't gone more than half a mile before a
bored-sounding voice boomed in through McCade's speakers.

"Hey, buddy, what the hell do you think you're doing?"

McCade felt his heart jump into his throat as he tried to
see where the voice was coming from. There it was about
a hundred feet away, a sleek, little four-place gig, complete
with an ugly-looking energy projector mounted in its bow.
Its approach had been hidden by the same rock he and Henry
had used. He swallowed hard.

"Doin'? I'm lookin' for a number three laser welder,
that's what I'm doin'. You haven't seen it, have you? Big
sucker with three tanks and a safety frame. Belongs to the
dockyard."

The same voice again. "I know what a number three laser

welder looks like, you blockhead. How did it get away?''

McCade added a whine to his voice. "It wasn't my fault, honest. Logan, he's the lead on my shift, he told me to bring him some insulation. When I went to get it, the welder just floated away."

"And he sent you out here looking for it?"

"That's right. Logan said to find it, or to plan on sucking some vacuum."

The voice laughed. "Well, buddy . . . the welder isn't likely to be this far out. And that being the case, I suggest you get your butt back toward the dock. Maybe next time you'll remember to rig a safety line. *Comprendez?*"

"*Comprendez*," McCade replied humbly as he took the controls from Henry. He put the sled into a long graceful turn and tried to figure out his next move.

A glance to the rear showed that the gig was still there. If they attempted to contact the non-existent Logan, he'd be well and truly screwed.

Turning forward, he saw something part company with the dockyard and move slowly his way. A ship! As it altered course and headed for the passageway, an idea started to form.

Looking back he saw the gig was gone. Good. Putting the sled on an intercepting course he mentally crossed his fingers. *If* the ship maintained its present course and speed, *if* its crew missed him on their scanners, and *if* the gig failed to reappear, his plan would work. It seemed like a lot of ifs.

Neither the ship nor the sled were moving very fast but their combined speed was fairly high. Given that, and given the fact that if he missed a head-on approach, he wouldn't get a second chance, McCade decided to come in from behind. That way it would be easier to match speeds and there would be less chance of being seen. When you're leaving port there's a natural tendency to look at what's up ahead rather than behind.

As he got closer McCade saw the ship was an armed merchantman. Chances were it had been captured and converted for use as a raider. He put the sled into a tight turn and gave chase. As he straightened the sled out, he saw that the raider was already pulling away from him.

McCade squeezed both handgrips and felt the sled surge forward. The forward motion pushed him into his seat and put pressure on some of his worst sore spots. McCade bit his lip and forced his mind back to the task at hand.

Up ahead the pirate ship grew steadily larger. If they maintained their present rate of speed, he'd be okay, but if they piled on some power, he'd be out of luck. The sled was going full out as it was, and if the pirates upped the ante, he'd never catch up. Not only that, but at the rate he was using nitrogen, he might not have enough to make the trip back.

Angling in to stay clear of the ship's drives, McCade held his breath. Now the raider was huge, blotting out the stars beyond, its black hull absorbing almost all the available light.

Dark though it was McCade saw that the hull was fairly smooth, typical of smaller ships that could negotiate planetary atmospheres, and far from ideal. While the smooth hull would help him land, it would also make him easier to see.

Closer . . . closer . . . almost there, now. The sled touched down with a gentle thump. McCade triggered the electromagnets embedded in its skids as the sled made contact with the ship's hull. The sled would remain locked in place as long as the power lasted.

"Nice job," Henry said in his ear. "Your navigation lacks a certain mathematical elegance, but it gets the job done."

"Thanks," McCade replied. "Now let's see if anyone noticed us getting aboard. Things might become somewhat unpleasant if they did."

Five minutes passed, ten minutes passed, and finally a full half hour passed. During this time the ship continued to accelerate toward the passage, and McCade began to relax. If the pirates hadn't spotted him by now, he figured they never would.

It felt good to relax. McCade felt suddenly tired. The hard work, the tension, and the succession of stim tabs seemed to catch up with him all at once. "Henry, I'm going to take a little nap. Wake me up when we're half an hour from the rendezvous point."

"You've got it, Sam," Henry replied cheerfully. "Sweet dreams . . . whatever dreams are."

McCade awoke with a struggle. It seemed as if he were far, far away, lost in some place where the air was sweet and his body didn't hurt. He wanted to stay there, tried to stay there, but the voice dragged him back.

"Sam, it's time to wake up, Sam . . ."

The first thing he noticed was the lack of vibration. The ship was gone and he was floating in space but where?

"We're at the rendezvous point," Henry said, anticipating his question. "Rather than wake you up I released the magnets and left the ship about ten standard hours ago."

"Ten standard hours . . ." McCade's eyes flew open. Ten standard hours plus, my God, damn near two days in the belt—what about his oxygen? McCade looked at the readout and saw that he was into the emergency reserve.

"What the hell are you doing, Henry? Why didn't you wake me? I'll be sucking vacuum in a few minutes."

"True," Henry said agreeably. "But I thought it would be rather cruel to wake you up just to point that out. Fortunately you don't need to worry. Take a look around."

McCade looked up and out. Ships. He was surrounded by ships. And not just any ships but a strange mix of vessels. Imperial destroyers next to Il Ronnian cruisers, next to— could it be? Yes, it looked as if the Brotherhood was represented as well, their ships being huddled together as if wary of the rest.

Then he heard Swanson-Pierce's familiar voice boom in

over his speakers. "Hello, Sam. While the sled suits your personality to a T, you might want something a little more substantial around you when the shooting starts. How about a drink and a good cigar?"

Twenty-seven

THE ASSAULT BOAT was brand-new. It looked new, it felt new, it even smelled new. McCade was doing his best to change that with a freshly lit cigar.

Reba wrinkled her nose from the copilot's seat and Neem coughed loudly from behind.

McCade didn't notice. Together with the fifty marines riding shotgun in the back, they were about to lead an assault on Pong's base, and his attention was focused on staying alive. As the first boat in, that would be difficult enough without any electronic or mechanical failures.

McCade scanned the indicator lights in groups. Hull integrity, locks sealed, no leaks. Drives on and green. Communications on and green. Jammers on and amber. Countermeasures on and amber. Chaff launchers on and amber. Weapons, primary and secondary, on and amber. They all looked good but McCade decided to cycle the boat's diagnostics one more time just to make sure.

"Henry, let's run the diagnostics one more time," McCade instructed. "If anything's belly up, let's find out about it now."

"That's a roger," Henry answered crisply. Henry had taken on a slightly military air ever since he'd been asked to download the assault path to the rest of the fleet's NAV-COMPs. Not satisfied to serve in any other boat, he'd disappeared into the control panel and taken over from the resident computer. What *it* thought of this arrangement nobody knew.

McCade checked the boat's main battle tank. The fleet made an impressive sight. It resembled a snake, shimmering with electronic scales, each one a ship. McCade's boat was located at the tip of the snake's nose, followed by a delta-shaped head full of interceptors and a long, thick body swarming with destroyers and cruisers.

It was a powerful force but a strange one. Behind his A-boat, Il Ronnian and Imperial interceptors jockeyed for position, each eager to lead the way, each determined to outshine the other.

Farther back pirate destroyers vied with Imperial cruisers for the honor of going in first while an Il Ronnian Star Sept Commander tried to pull rank on both.

It was one of the strangest military alliances ever put together and a rather temporary one at that. The Imperial Navy was attempting to avoid a galactic war, the Il Ronnians were trying to recover the Vial of Tears, and the Brotherhood was afraid of getting caught in the middle. And everyone would go their separate ways the moment their objectives were achieved.

In the meantime the partnership made sense.

Methuselah had practically fallen out of hyperspace seconds ahead of a major control systems failure. Fortunately the old ship emerged almost on top of the Imperial naval base that the Geezer had been instructed to find. Hours later *Methuselah* was in the friendly grasp of a naval tug and on its way to the Kodula Naval Base.

Once in orbit Neem and Reba were rushed down to the surface where they were interviewed by the base commander. And much to Reba's amazement Commander Moreno took their story seriously, fired off a message torp to sector headquarters, and began to organize the few forces she had available.

Like every other senior officer within Imperial space, Moreno had orders to provide someone named Sam McCade with anything he wanted. And the *anything* had been underlined.

The orders didn't mention pirates and Il Ronnians, but Moreno lumped them under *anything* and did what they asked. That included provision of two message torpedoes that were launched toward destinations outside of Imperial space.

Doing so required a certain amount of professional courage on Moreno's part, courage that was severely tested when a small fleet of Il Ronnian ships suddenly left hyperspace and dropped into orbit around her planet.

Within a few minutes the alien was busy gabbing with an Il Ronnian big shot named Teeb, her XO was on the verge of having a heart attack, and Moreno was wondering if she'd committed a serious error.

Fortunately the next group of ships to arrive brought Admiral Swanson-Pierce with them. Otherwise the subsequent manifestation of pirate ships would have shaken even Moreno's considerable poise.

But Swanson-Pierce listened to Moreno's report, promoted her to full captain, and proceeded to invite the senior members of all three groups to dinner.

After a report by the Reba woman and the Il Ronnian civilian, everyone agreed to a joint assault on Pong's base and hoisted a few to seal the bargain. It was then that Moreno learned that Il Ronnians can not only handle alcohol, they can do so in prodigious quantities.

Now the mixed fleet was awaiting orders from a cashiered naval officer/bounty hunter who claimed to know a secret passage through the thickest part of the Nakasoni Asteroid Belt. If it wasn't the craziest thing Moreno had ever heard of, it certainly ran a close second. However there was no sign of these thoughts on her handsome face when she turned to Admiral Swanson-Pierce and gave her report.

"There's still a little squabbling toward the rear of the formation, Admiral, but ninety percent of our units are where they're supposed to be, and all things considered that's pretty good. We stand ready to attack on your command."

For a naval officer who was about to risk his career on what most of his peers would consider an insane mission, Swanson-Pierce looked very relaxed. He leaned back in his command chair and smiled. "Not this time, Captain. This is McCade's show, and he won't raise the curtain without an attempt to irritate me first."

Unlike McCade's cramped assault boat, the bridge of the cruiser *Tenacious* was both spacious and comfortable. Pilots, electronic warfare specialists, and weapons officers tended their various boards with the quiet reverence of priests before an altar. All wore space armor in case of a sudden loss of cabin pressure.

A com tech appeared at Moreno's side. "I've got a com call from A-boat One on channel three, Admiral. Will you take it?"

Swanson-Pierce grinned at Moreno. "See?"

Then he turned back to the tech. "Put McCade through by all means."

"Aye, aye, sir."

Seconds later one of the four com screens mounted in front of Swanson-Pierce lit up and Sam McCade appeared. There was a half-smoked cigar clenched between his teeth and he was in dire need of a shave.

"Hello, Walt. Well, I never thought I'd say it, but for once your people seem to have their shit together. My compliments to Commander Moreno. According to Reba she's real sharp, although I find that hard to believe, since really sharp people avoid your chicken-shit outfit like the plague."

"It's *Captain* Moreno now," Swanson-Pierce replied dryly. "And I'll give her your message."

"Thanks," McCade replied, removing the cigar from his mouth and rubbing it out on the heretofore spotless control console. "Now, if you naval types are done polishing your posteriors, we can get this show on the road."

"Lead the way, Sam, we'll be right behind you."

"That's just great," McCade replied sourly. "Try not to blow my ass off." And with that the screen faded to black.

"He really *is* obnoxious," Moreno said wonderingly.

"Yup," Swanson-Pierce replied cheerfully. "And as Mustapha Pong's about to learn, you haven't seen anything yet."

McCade turned to look at Neem. Since his tail was enclosed by his space armor, the Il Ronnian gave him a human thumbs-up, as did Sergeant Major Valarie Sibo. Her marines were out of sight in the main compartment but their status lights were solid green.

"All right, Henry, take us in at full military speed."

The boxy-looking assault boat wasn't pretty but it was fast. As Henry goosed the boat's dual drives, McCade flipped all the weapons systems from amber to full green. After that he enabled all the automatic defensive systems, opened his visor, and lit a cigar. Even at high speed they wouldn't hit the first sensor station for another two hours.

He was just leaning back in his seat when every alarm on the board lit up, went off, or printed out. A single glance at the main battle tank told the story. Two of Pong's ships were on their way out!

He'd known it was possible but hadn't really expected it to happen. Damn!

Cigar ash dribbled down across the front of McCade's armor as he slapped the emergency attack bar and felt the boat jerk in response.

The WEAPCOMP had a flat, emotionless voice. "Two torpedoes away and running, two ship-to-ship missiles in flight, chaff left, chaff left, closing, closing. Target one is full evasive, target is full evasive, jamming, jamming full spectrum all freq's.

"Both targets have launched defensive missiles, closing, closing, torpedo two has been neutralized, missiles one and two neutralized, we have a hit from torpedo one on target two. Target two destroyed. Target one has launched four missiles, tracking, tracking . . ."

McCade was thrown on his side as the boat banked right and then left.

Henry did his best to take evasive action as the WEAP-COMP continued its dispassionate narration. "Chaff left, chaff right, full spectrum electro countermeasures engaged, defensive missiles, launch, launch. Target one is approaching effective range of secondary weapons, fire, fire, target engaged and returning fire . . ."

The boat shuddered as Henry jinked right, left, and right again.

McCade fought the G forces and did his best to follow the action in the battle tank. Suddenly two green deltas appeared on either side of the red circle that marked the A-boat's position.

"We have side by side friendlies," the WEAPCOMP droned on, "launching, launching. Target one has launched full spectrum defensive, closing, closing, hit, hit, hit, miss. Friendly one has a hit on target one. Target one destroyed. Load, load, all systems cycled to full green."

McCade brought his hand up to wipe the sweat off his forehead and found a cigar butt between his gloved fingers. Making a fist he crushed it out. He chinned his mike.

"Is everyone okay?"

"We took some hits from flying debris," Reba observed, "but the armor handled most of it. We did lose our backup antenna array however."

"Could've been a lot worse," McCade replied. "Neem, how are the passengers doing?"

"Pretty well, Sam. The sergeant major's taking a nap, and the rest of her team is taking bets on whether Private Mahowski will throw up in his helmet or shit his pants."

McCade grinned. Marines are resourceful if nothing else.

Two hours later they hit the first sensor station. It had a fraction of a second to see the assault boat, the wave of interceptors behind it, and squirt a message toward Pong's base. Then the WEAPCOMP launched a single missile and the station was gone, leaving nothing more than a pool of cooling metal to mark the place where it had once stood.

But the sensor station had accomplished its mission. And when its message flashed into the *Earth Star*'s com center, the duty officer wasted no time in taking action.

His name was Farb. He was a slender man with close-cropped blond hair and a predatory face. The prospect of some action made him smile. He thumbed a red button.

All over the ship gongs began to clang, lights began to flash, and thousands of people ran for their action stations.

Electronic signals flashed out, were verified, and immediately acted on. Destroyers and cruisers and interceptors took up their various positions and prepared for battle.

As all of this took place Farb calmly made his way down a broad corridor, past row after row of first-class cabins, and paused in front of a massive hatch. It was made of durasteel bonded to gold and had once opened to admit the Emperor himself.

Farb palmed the entry lock and waited for Pong's voice. "Yes?"

"Detector Station One reports a large force of heavily armed intruders. We have confirmation from stations two, three, and four. ETA . . . twenty minutes."

There was a moment of silence before Pong replied. "Our ships?"

"Dispersed according to plan two," Farb replied. "Orders?"

"Pipe all incoming data to the tank in my quarters. All ships will fight to the death. Remind them that there's no other way out."

"It shall be as you wish," Farb answered.

Just as he was turning to leave, Pong spoke once more. "And, Farb . . ."

"Yes?"

"You'd better have someone prepare the *Arrow*."

Farb grinned. The *Arrow* was Pong's private yacht. Should things go poorly, Pong, Farb, and two other trusted lieutenants would use it to make their escape. Although very few people knew about it, there *was* another way out.

McCade and everyone else aboard the assault boat very nearly died as they passed between Pong's weapons emplacements.

A bright latticework of coherent energy webbed across the passageway threatening to wrap the boat in its lethal embrace. Missiles accelerated from launchers searching for heat and metal. Other missiles leaped from the boat's rotary launchers to meet those missiles as still more missiles came up to meet them.

Walls of flame erupted as waves of missiles intersected and canceled each other out. Torpedoes followed the tons of hot chaff that the invading ships scattered across the passageway, exploding whenever they came near. And everywhere electronic signals raced, probed, and tried to fake each other out.

Inside the boat they were thrown up, down, and back and forth as Henry tried to keep them alive and the WEAPCOMP droned on. It spoke of torpedoes, missiles, and targets as if they were somewhere else, distant things that were part of someone else's world.

One by one the interceptors assigned to guard them blossomed into flowers of flame and disappeared. It was brute strength against brute strength, missile against missile, computer against computer.

McCade grit his teeth and willed the weapons emplacements to die. And one by one they did die, each wave of passing ships pounding them further into submission, until none were left.

McCade chinned his mike as the A-boat flashed into Pong's inner sphere. "Assault Boat One to Assault Leader."

"We copy, Assault Boat One," a voice answered. "Go".

McCade imagined Swanson-Pierce sitting in his command chair listening to the conversation. The bastard was probably sipping a cup of tea or something.

"Phase one is complete, Assault Leader. Confirm phase two."

"Phase two confirmed, Boat One," the voice said. "You have new friendlies port and starboard, with ground pounders bringing up the rear. Assault Leader sends 'well done.' "

"Copy that," McCade replied sourly. "Tell the Assault Leader to come up and join us."

A glance at the battle tank showed that a swarm of fresh interceptors had formed up around him. They were followed by a gaggle of boxy A-boats. Each boat held fifty marines.

The interceptors would attempt to punch a hole through the pirate defense allowing the A-boats to close with and board the *Earth Star*. Once aboard they'd try to find the Vial of Tears, and failing that, Mustapha Pong.

Meanwhile the combined force of destroyers and cruisers would move in and fight the main battle. McCade grinned at the thought. Wait till Pong's people got a load of those Il Ronnian warships!

McCade chinned his mike. "This is Boat One. Let's kick some butt."

Henry's response threw McCade back and down. He forced his head toward the battle tank. A whole wave of ships and interceptors were coming toward him. He felt an anvil hit the bottom of his stomach. He thought of Sara and Molly, then thought no more as the boat went into a jerky pattern of evasive maneuvers.

What followed happened too quickly for human hands or eyes to follow. It was a computer war of launch and counterlaunch, jam and counterjam, move and countermove.

Whether you lived or died depended on the speed and quality of your computers, upon the effectiveness of your weapons, and on that most fickle of all things, luck.

But their plan worked. Even though Pong's warships were *supposed* to defend the *Earth Star*, many of them were actually trying to escape instead. An attack by the Brotherhood was one thing, but an attack by a combined force of pirate, navy, and alien ships was something else again. They wanted out.

The pirate ships were like a long, thin wall of metal, a

tough obstacle to get around, but a relatively easy one to punch through. And that's what the interceptors did.

By concentrating all their firepower on a single point, the interceptors managed to overwhelm two destroyers and a light cruiser, making a hole through which the A-boats could pass.

The *Earth Star* had weapons of her own, but like most liners her defenses were more symbolic than real and were soon neutralized by the swarming interceptors.

"Put us alongside that emergency lock," McCade ordered as he sealed his visor. "And somebody wake the sergeant major."

"That won't be necessary, sir," Sergeant Major Sibo replied calmly. "Just put this crate alongside and we'll do the rest."

The sergeant major was as good as her word. McCade had pumped all the atmosphere out of the cabin by the time Henry put the A-boat alongside the larger ship. As a result there was no time wasted matching locks. Armed with a ship cracker it took three marines ten minutes to cut their way through the *Star*'s outer hatch.

McCade knew that other teams were using the same strategy all over the ship. If nothing else that would force Pong's crew to split up into smaller groups and make them easier to handle.

A large piece of hull metal came free and spun off into space. A satchel charge flew into the open lock and exploded with a brilliant flash. Armored bodies followed it in, their blast rifles burping blue light.

Sergeant Major Sibo's voice dominated the command channel for the next few minutes. "Spread out, you idiots! One grenade'll get you all. What's the matter, Mahowski? Afraid to earn your pay? Shoot those bastards before they shoot you. Wu, you idiot, get your head down before they blow it off. Great Sol, have I gotta wipe your ass too?"

Then it was over and she was in the blackened lock urging McCade to board. "The lock's secure, sir, welcome aboard."

"Thank you, Sergeant Major, nicely done. Have you got the schematic?"

"Yes, sir. It's up on my visor right now."

"Good, let's head for the Imperial stateroom. If Pong's aboard, that's where he'll be."

"Aye, aye, sir," Sibo replied. "Follow me."

McCade followed and was forced to step over a number of bodies in the process. At least two of them wore marine armor.

With Reba and Neem close behind him, McCade followed Sibo through a short side passage to the point where it joined a main corridor. Another lock blocked their way. An indicator showed breathable atmosphere beyond. At the sergeant major's direction four marines cycled through and signaled the all-clear.

As she emerged from the lock, Sibo took a moment to consult her schematic and turned left. Two marines brushed past her to take the point as the rest of them formed a column of twos and jogged along behind.

Like all liners the schematics for the *Earth Star* were on file at every navy base. That was SOP in case of collision or capture. So as each team of marines made their way on board they'd use the schematics projected onto the inside surface of their visors to find their particular targets. Strategic targets came first, like the bridge, the com center, and the drive rooms, followed by storerooms or other places where the Vial of Tears might be stored.

At least one Il Ronnian Sand Sept trooper had been assigned to each team of marines. Once the vial was found the Sand Sept trooper would stand guard over it until one of the several Ilwiks present could take possession.

The journey soon became a running firefight as the marines encountered small groups of crew members and quickly overwhelmed them. Pong did have some well-trained troops, but most of them were aboard his destroyers and cruisers, and therefore unavailable to defend the *Star*.

The marines were able to make good progress as a result.

Slowly but surely they made their way ever toward the first-class accommodations and the Imperial stateroom.

Then, just as they left a side corridor to enter the main thoroughfare that led to the Imperial stateroom, they hit an ambush.

Farb had placed his people well, hiding them in two opposing staterooms and an overhead access tunnel. Holding his breath he waited for the marines to pass and yelled "Now!" into his open mike.

The pirates opened up from both sides as more dropped from above to block any possibility of retreat.

Sergeant Major Sibo died in the first five seconds of the ambush, slumping forward as a crew-operated energy beam punched black holes through her armor.

McCade hit the deck in a forward roll. As he came out of it his hand blaster jumped into his hand. Pirates spilled out of a stateroom to the left. He squeezed the trigger four times and saw two holes appear in a visor that quickly misted over with blood.

Something hit his armor from behind but didn't go through. McCade spun around and gut shot a pirate from three feet away.

Tough though it was the pirate's armor couldn't stand up to that kind of punishment and gave way. The energy beam went through Farb's stomach and splashed against the back-side of his armor. The ensuing darkness came as a complete surprise.

Suddenly it was over and the marines had won. Bodies lay everywhere in tumbled heaps. A blue haze filled the air and when McCade opened his visor the smell of ozone filled his nostrils.

A marine appeared at his side. "Sergeant O'Hara, sir. We have sixteen dead, seven wounded, and twenty-seven effectives. Orders, sir?"

McCade could see the golden hatch at the far end of the corridor. "See that hatch, Sergeant? I want it open."

"Open. Yes, sir. Rawlings! Newly! Mobutu! Open up

that door and make it quick. The rest of you, cover them. We may run into all sorts of shit in there.''

Half a minute later the three marines were busy cutting their way through the hatch. The ship cracker spit ruby red and the hatch sucked it up until the locking mechanism gave way and the door began to slide open.

The marines dropped the ship cracker and scrambled to get out of the way. Thirty weapons were lined up on the open hatch but nothing happened.

"Okay," McCade said, "let's take it nice n'easy."

As the marines moved forward, Reba slipped in from the side. Blue light stuttered out to lance through her body in a dozen places. McCade watched in utter amazement as she brought up her blast rifle and fired back. There was a double thump as two pirates hit the floor.

McCade ran forward and was there to catch her when she fell. White fluid spurted from the holes in her armor. He couldn't place it at first and then he could and didn't want to believe it. Holding her in his arms, McCade looked up at Neem, and when the Il Ronnian nodded, he knew it was true. Reba was, and always had been, a cyborg. As such she'd infiltrated the Brotherhood, been accidentally captured, and been reinfiltrated via her association with McCade. Her voice made a horrible rasping sound when she spoke.

"Sam?"

"Yes, Reba?"

"I'm sorry I lied to you."

"It's okay, Reba. I understand."

"Sam . . . are you really an Ilwik?"

McCade looked up at Neem and he nodded.

"Yes, Reba, I guess I am."

"Good," Reba rasped. "Then give me the prayer for the dead."

The words tumbled from McCade's lips as if he'd said them many times before. "You may leave this one, O holy fluid, for your work is done. She has lived fully, seen much, and served with honor. Now she journeys forth into a new land where you await. Our blessings go with her for she was one of ours.

"Was that okay, Reba? Did I say it right?"

But Reba was silent, her beautiful features frozen in a smile.

Neem pulled McCade to his feet. "It was more than okay, Sam. It was perfect. Now come on before Reba blows up and takes you with her."

McCade was leaning against a wall and looking the other way when Reba blew up. He was tired of killing, and tired of watching people die. No matter how hard he willed his body to move, it wouldn't go. He dimly heard Sergeant O'Hara give the all-clear and heard the marines spread out to search the stateroom.

Pong was gone, of course, having escaped along with two others aboard his yacht, but Neem found something of interest on the surface of the pirate's rather ornate desk. Pong had used it as a paperweight and, being of little intrinsic value, had neglected to take it along.

The object was made of purest crystal and shaped like a vial. Inside the vial a clear fluid could be seen. It was moving. With life of its own? Or in sympathy with the ship?

In either case the vial shimmered with light and threw a rainbow of color against the wall beyond as Neem picked it up and said a silent prayer.

With trembling hands Neem carried the vial into the adjoining room and to the place where the tired-looking human stood. Placing the vial in McCade's hands, Neem said, "The Vial of Tears, O holy one." And together the Ilwiks cried.